Can I Have a Turn?

ACORN™
SCHOLASTIC INC.

Norm Feuti

For Charlotte and Ben —NF

Library of Congress Cataloging-in-Publication Data

Names: Feuti, Norman, author, illustrator.
Title: Can I have a turn? / Norm Feuti.
Description: First edition. | New York : Acorn/Scholastic Inc., 2022. |
Series: Hello, Hedgehog! ; 5 | Summary: After Harry receives a new toy car in the mail, Harry and Hedgehog have fun taking turns racing the car around the racetrack Harry built.
Identifiers: LCCN 2021001276 (print) | ISBN 9781338677140 (paperback) |
ISBN 9781338677157 (library binding) |
Subjects: CYAC: Hedgehogs—Fiction. | Sharing—Fiction. | Toys—Fiction. |
Friendship—Fiction.
Classification: LCC PZ7.1.F52 Can 2022 (print) |
DDC [E]—dc23

LC record available at https://lccn.loc.gov/2021001276

10 9 8 7 6 5 4 3 2 1   22 23 24 25 26

Printed in China   62
First edition, February 2022
Edited by Katie Carella
Book design by Maria Mercado

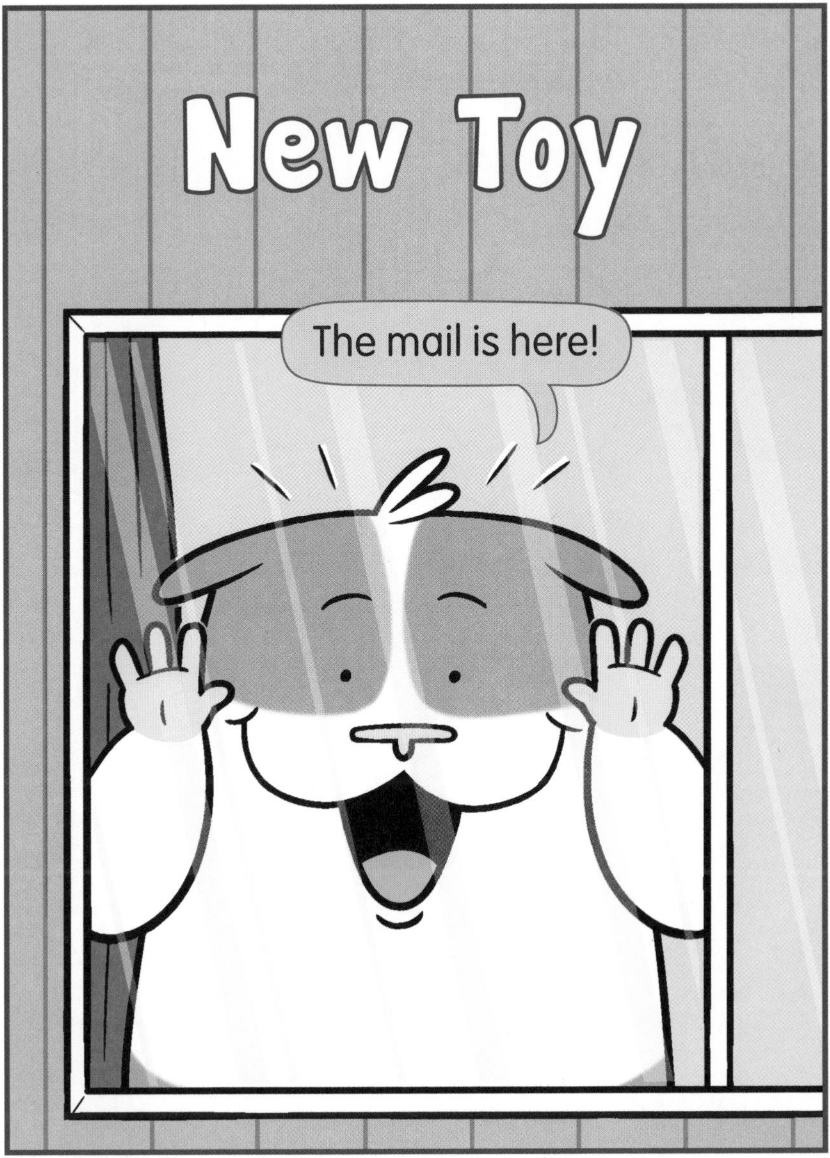
New Toy
The mail is here!

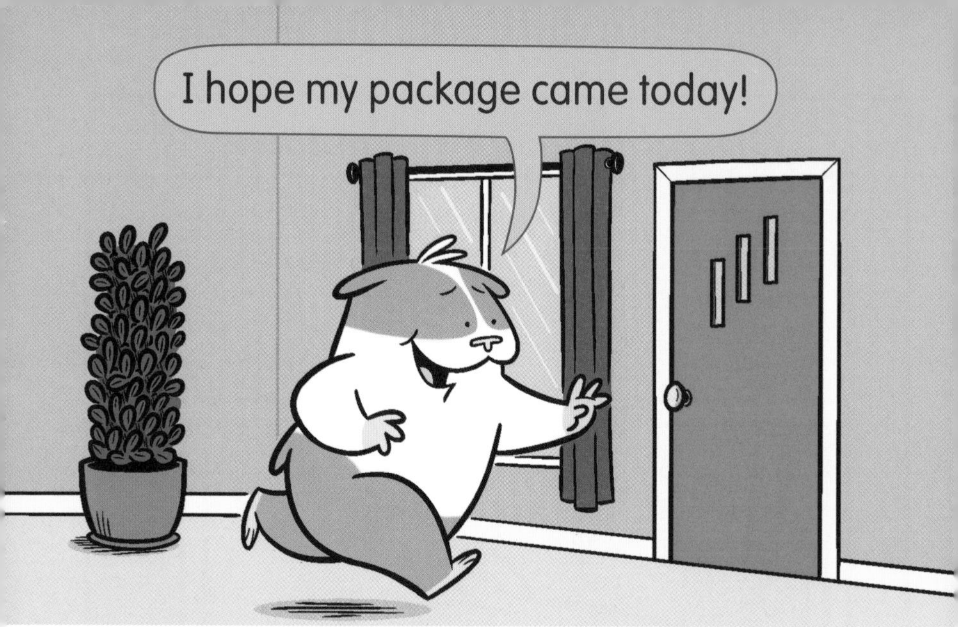
I hope my package came today!

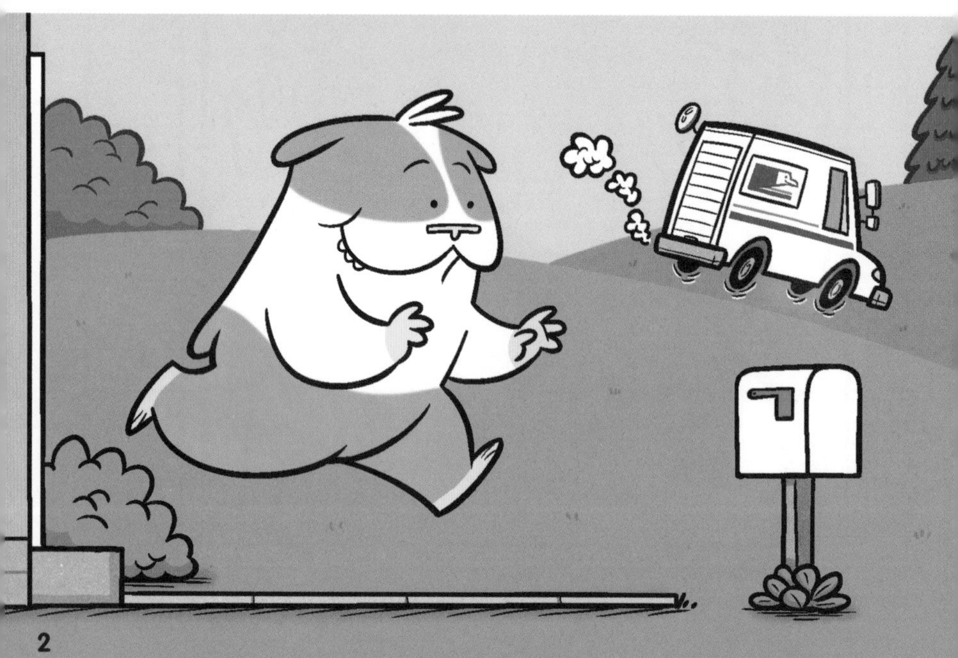

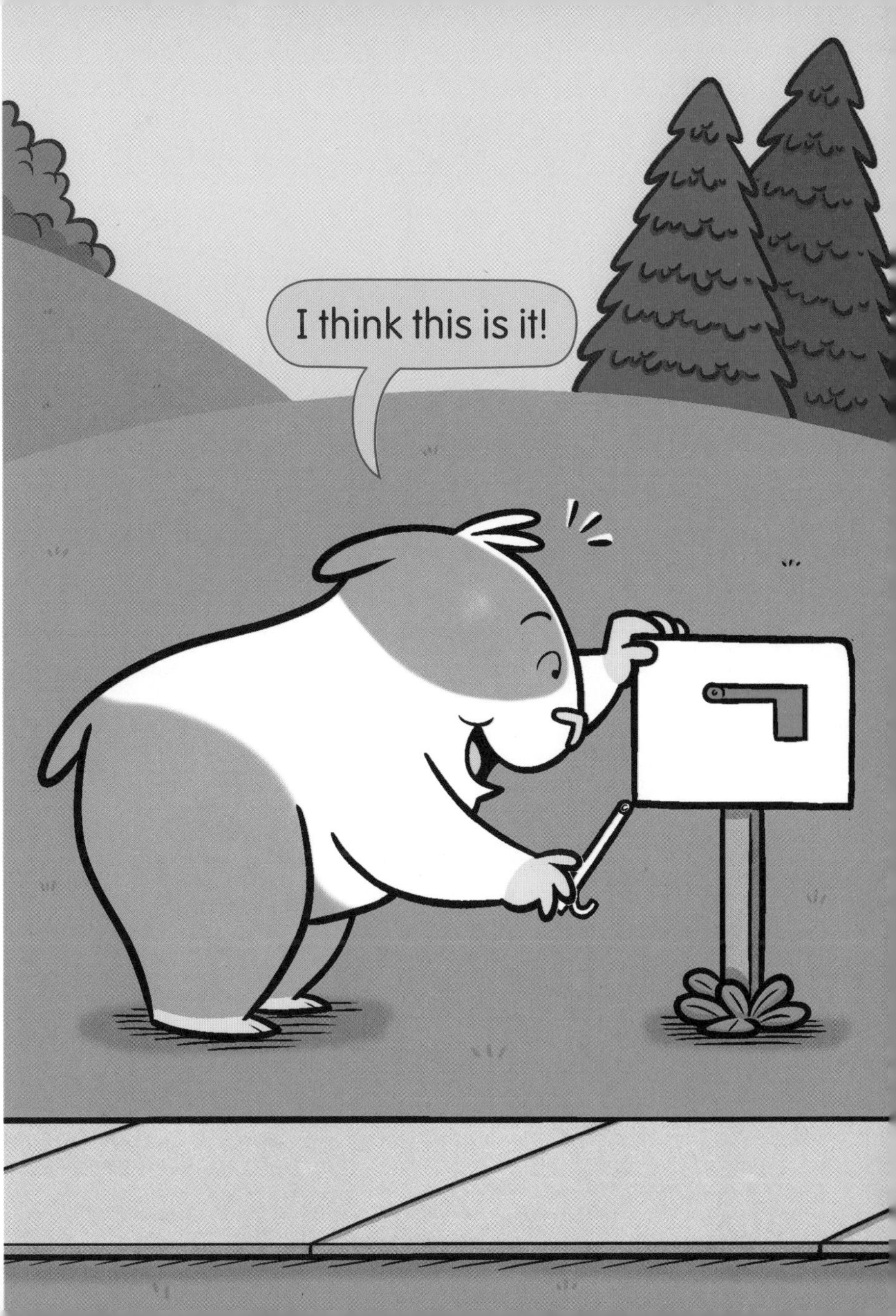
I think this is it!

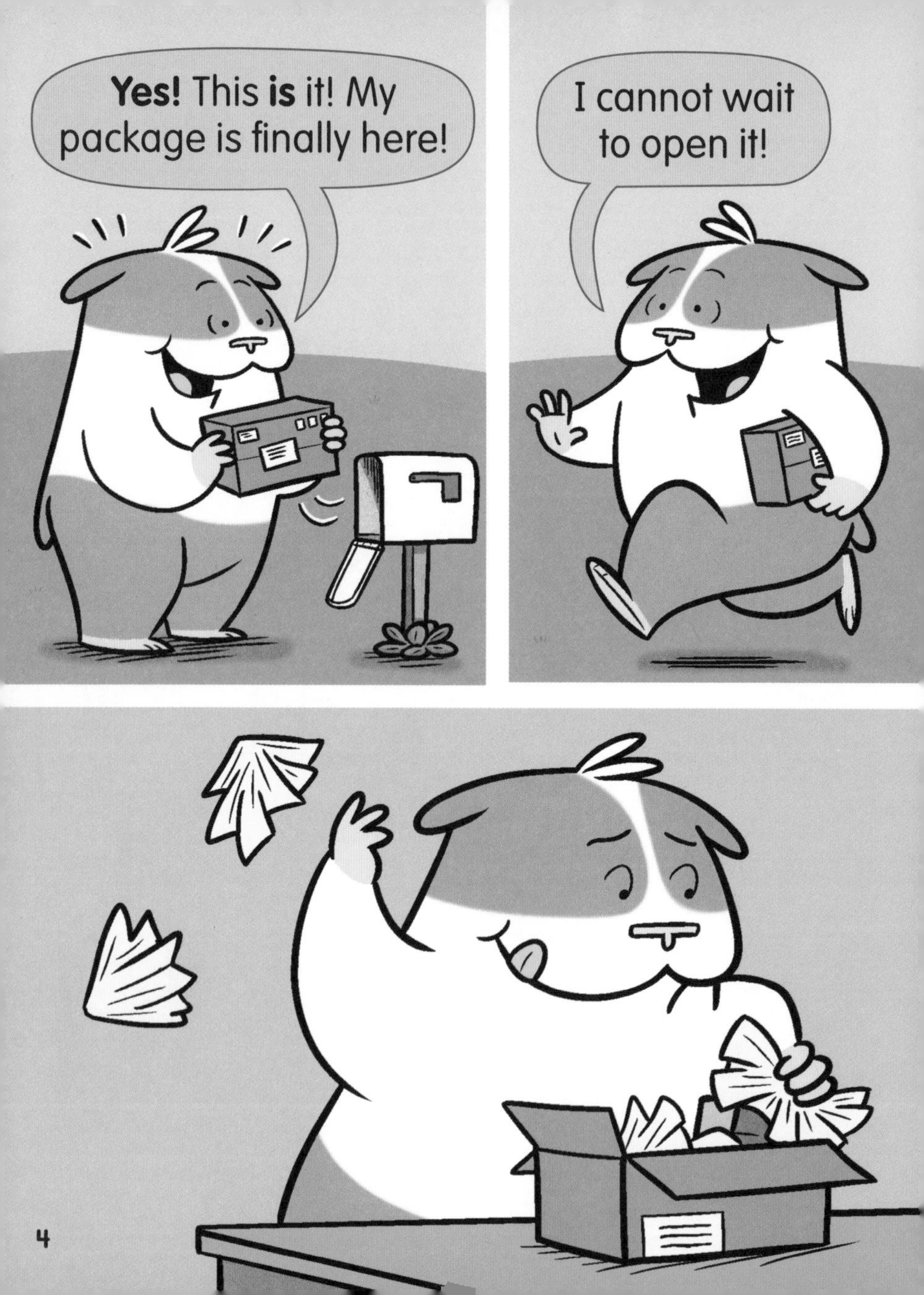
Yes! This **is** it! My package is finally here!
I cannot wait to open it!

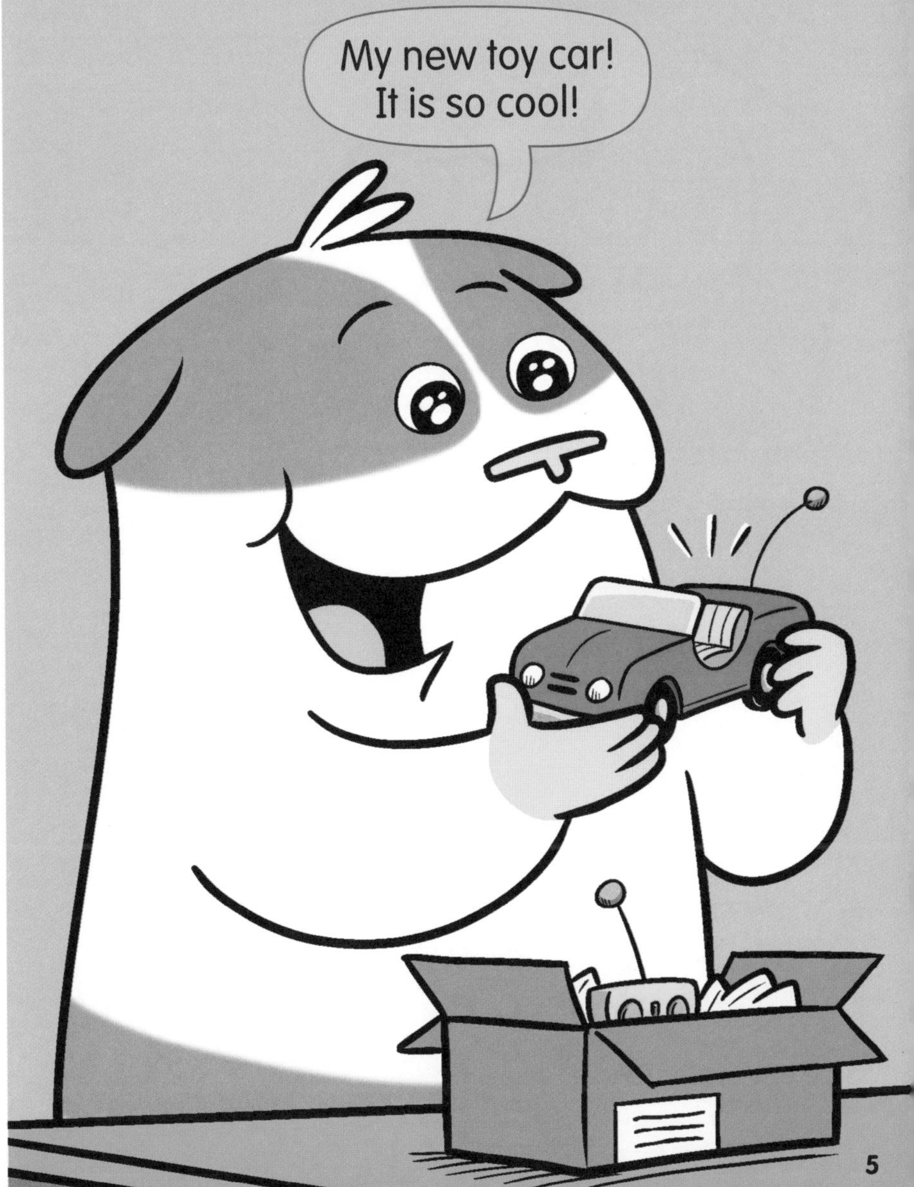
My new toy car!
It is so cool!

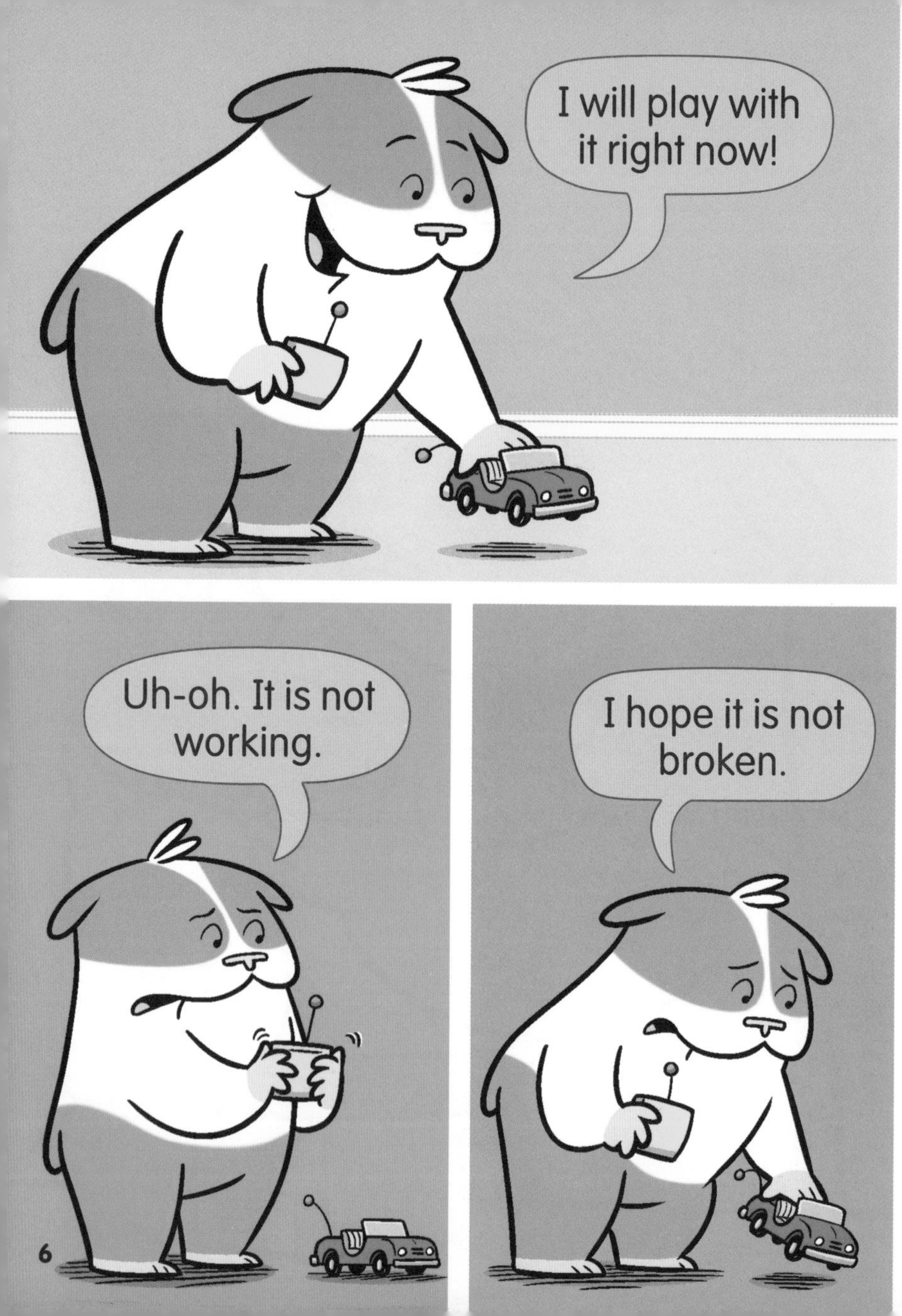
I will play with it right now!
Uh-oh. It is not working.
I hope it is not broken.

Oh. It needs batteries to work.

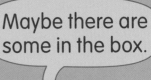

Maybe there are some in the box.

Oh no. It did not come with batteries.

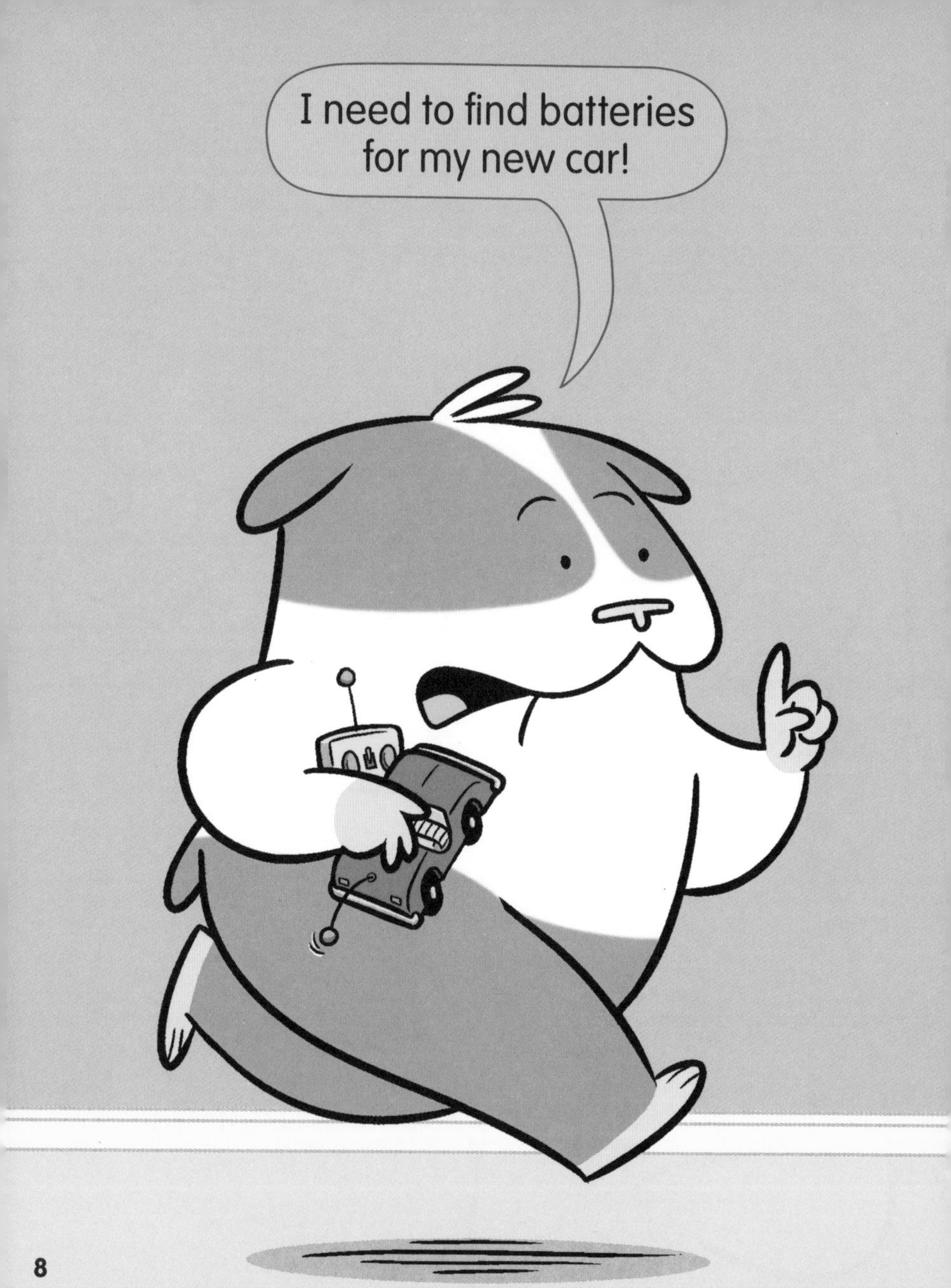
I need to find batteries for my new car!

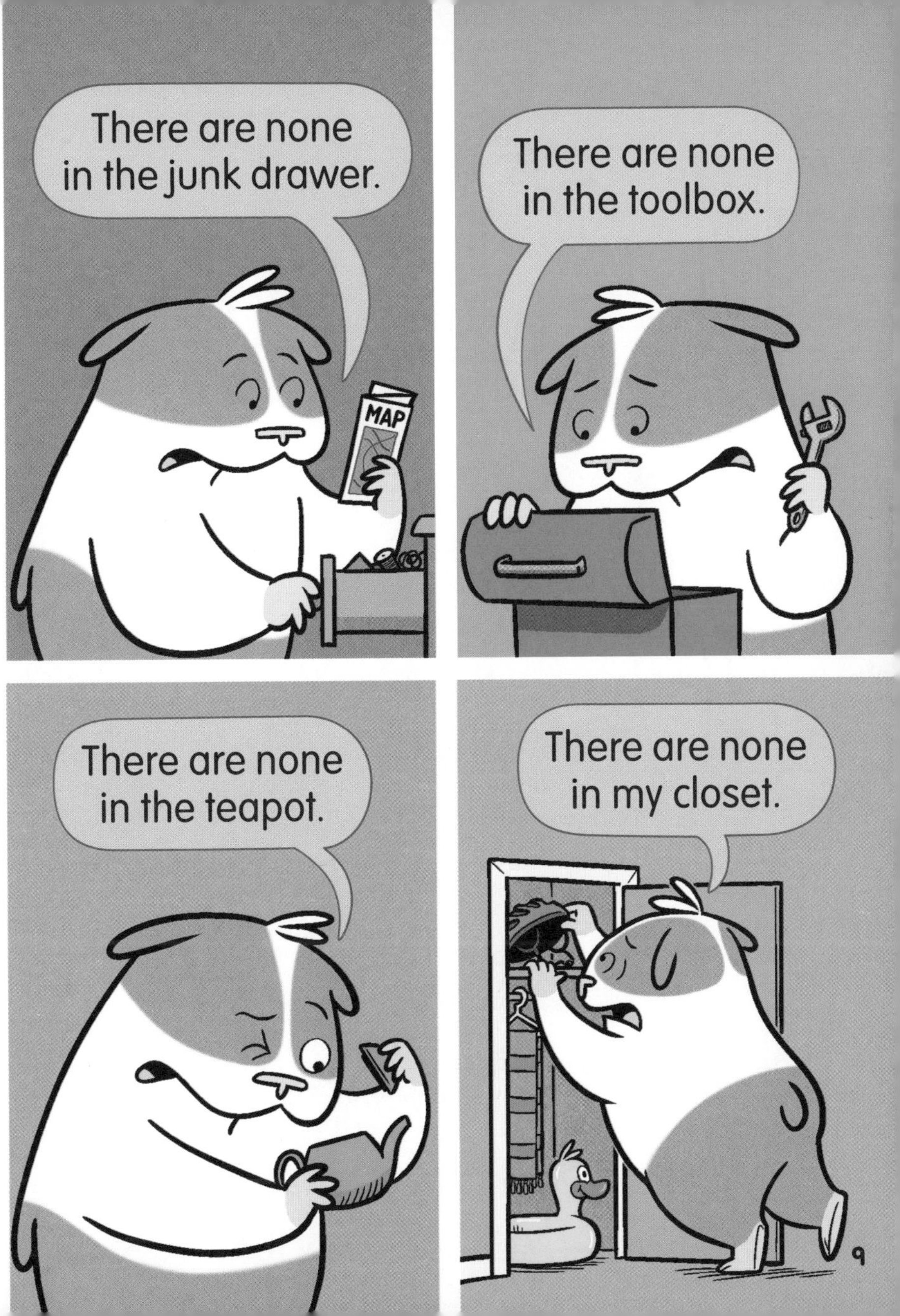
There are none in the junk drawer.
MAP
There are none in the toolbox.
There are none in the teapot.
There are none in my closet.

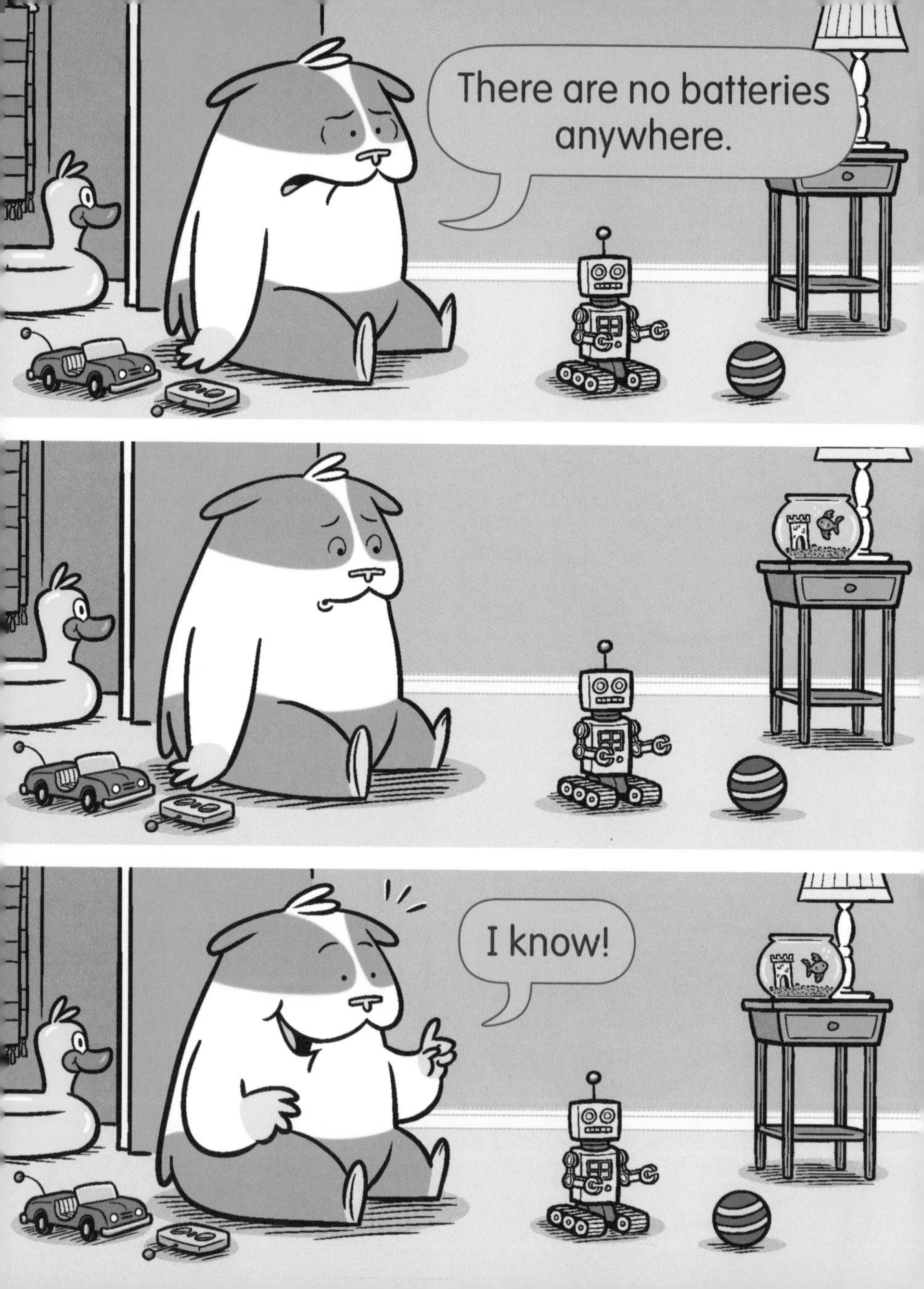
There are no batteries anywhere.
I know!

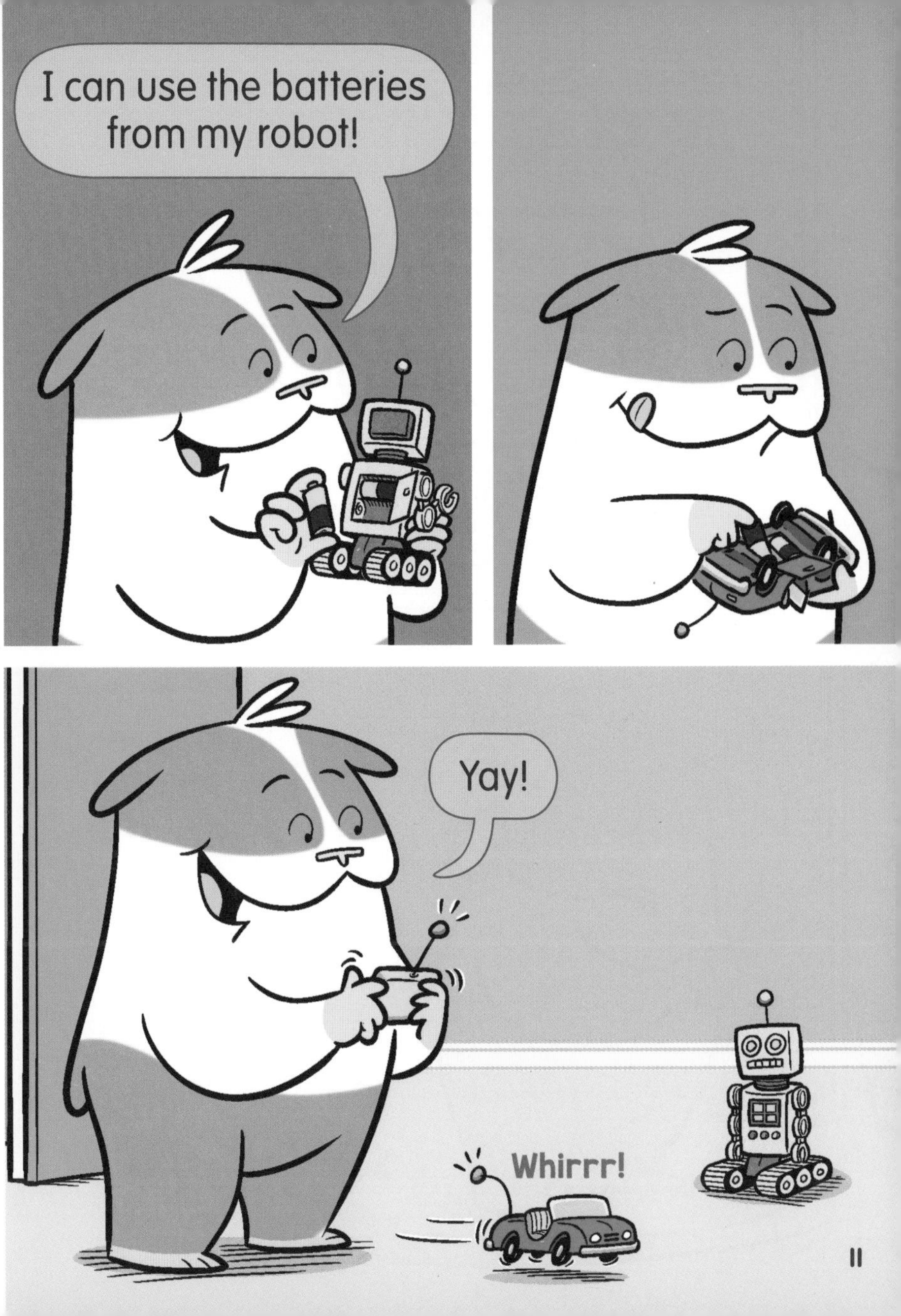
I can use the batteries from my robot!
Yay!
Whirrr!

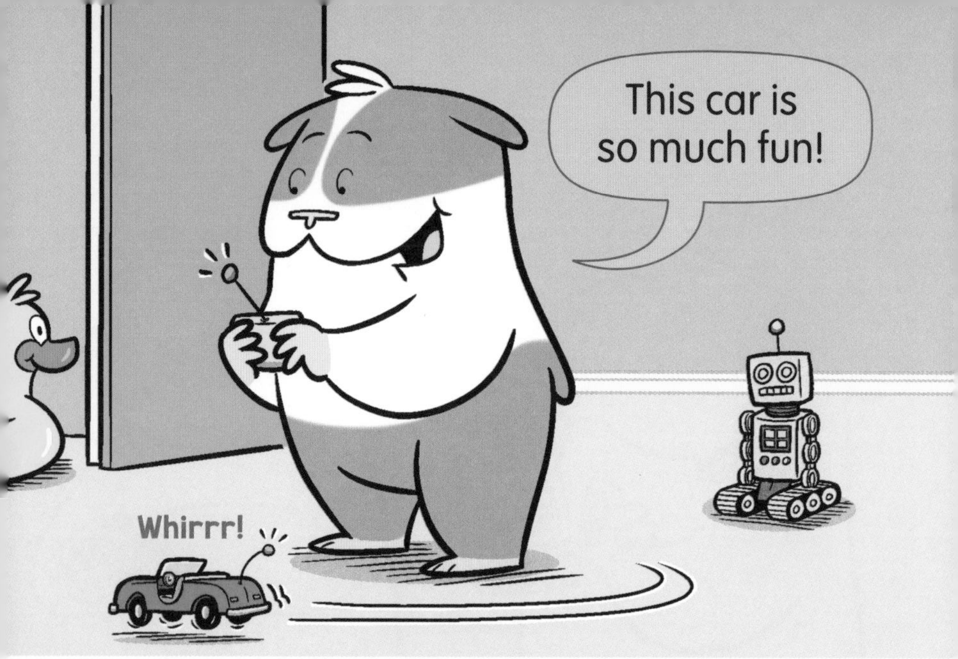

This car is so much fun!
Whirrr!

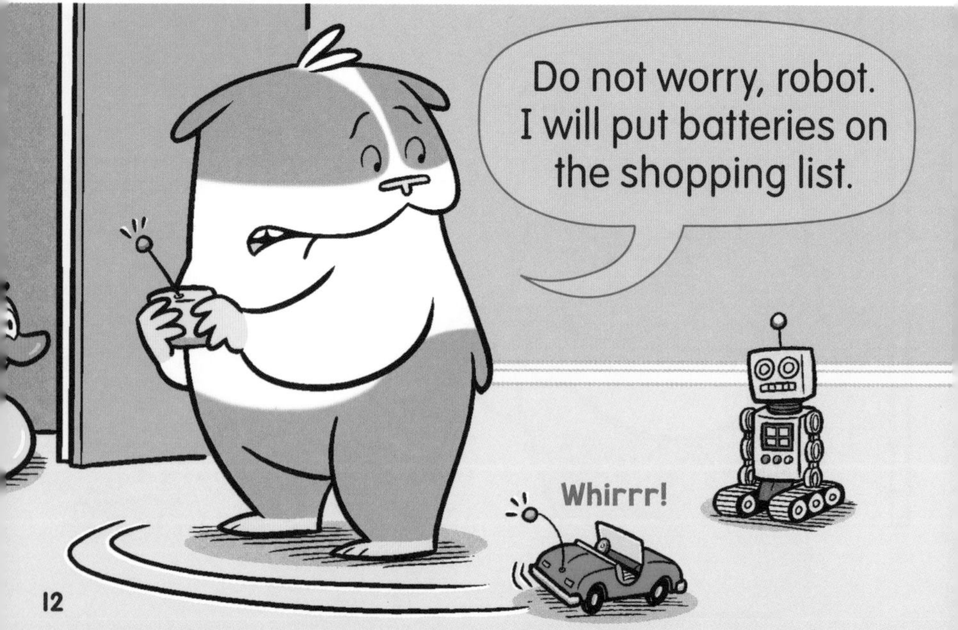

Do not worry, robot. I will put batteries on the shopping list.
Whirrr!

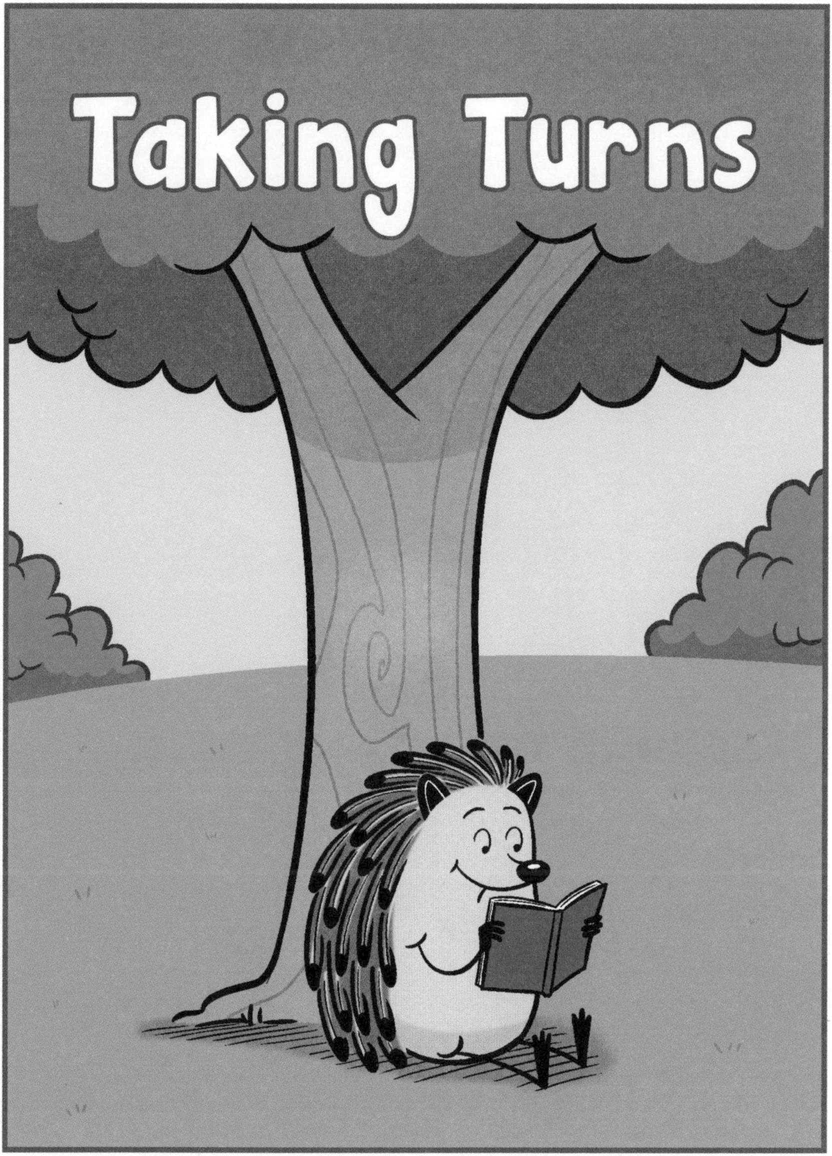
Taking Turns

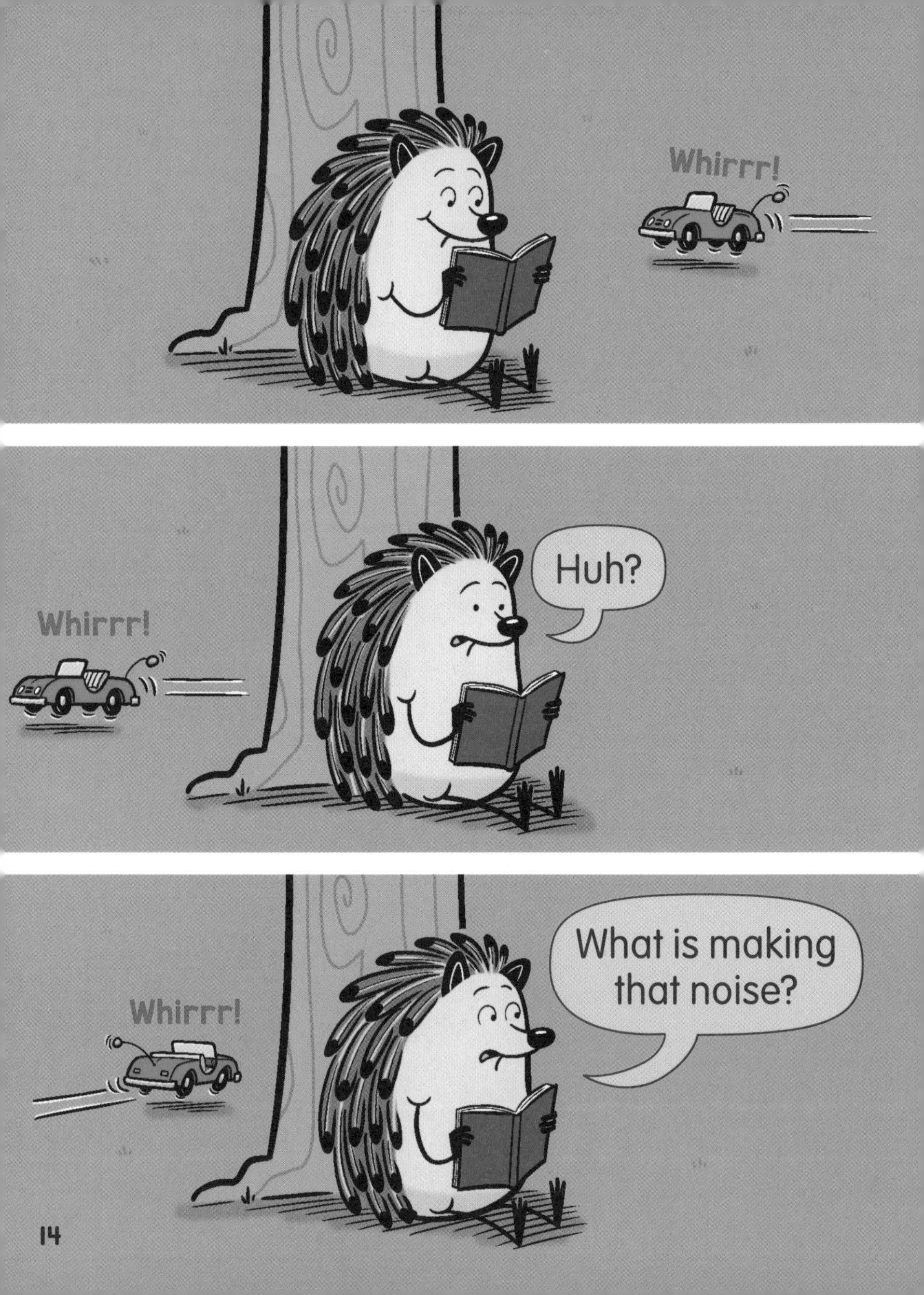
Whirrr!
Whirrr!
Huh?
Whirrr!
What is making that noise?

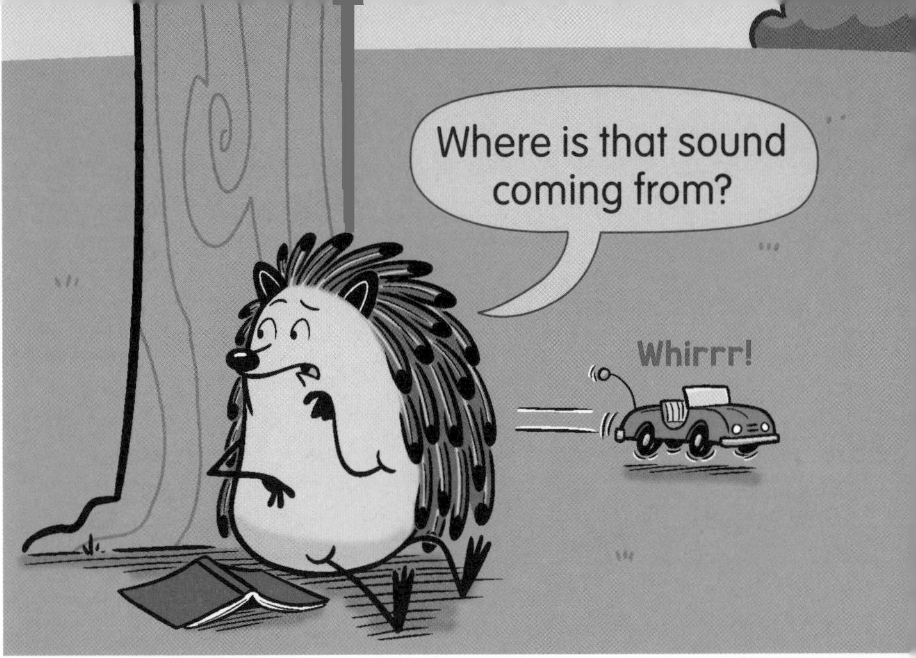
Where is that sound coming from?
Whirrr!

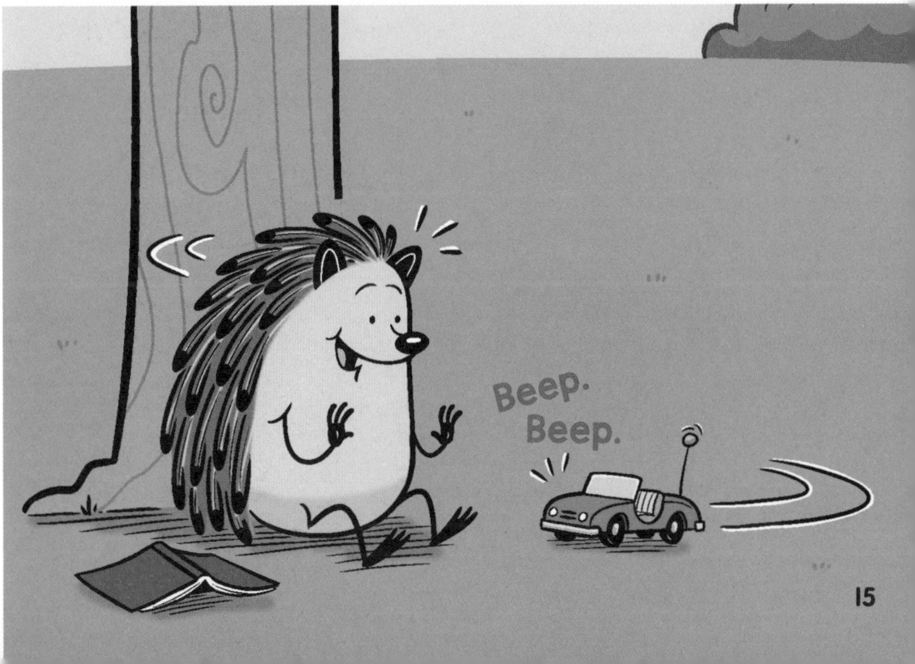
Beep.
Beep.

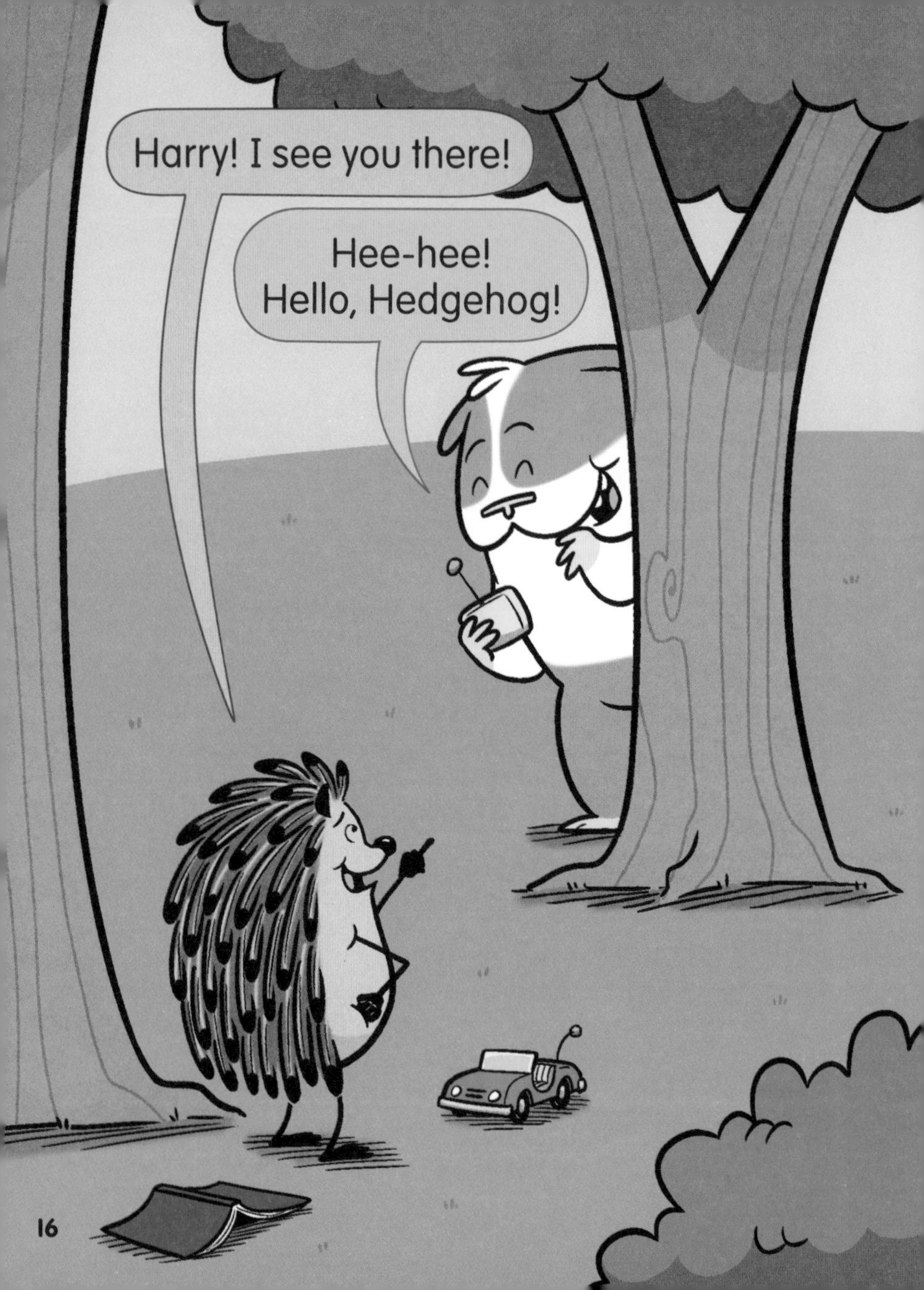
Harry! I see you there!
Hee-hee! Hello, Hedgehog!

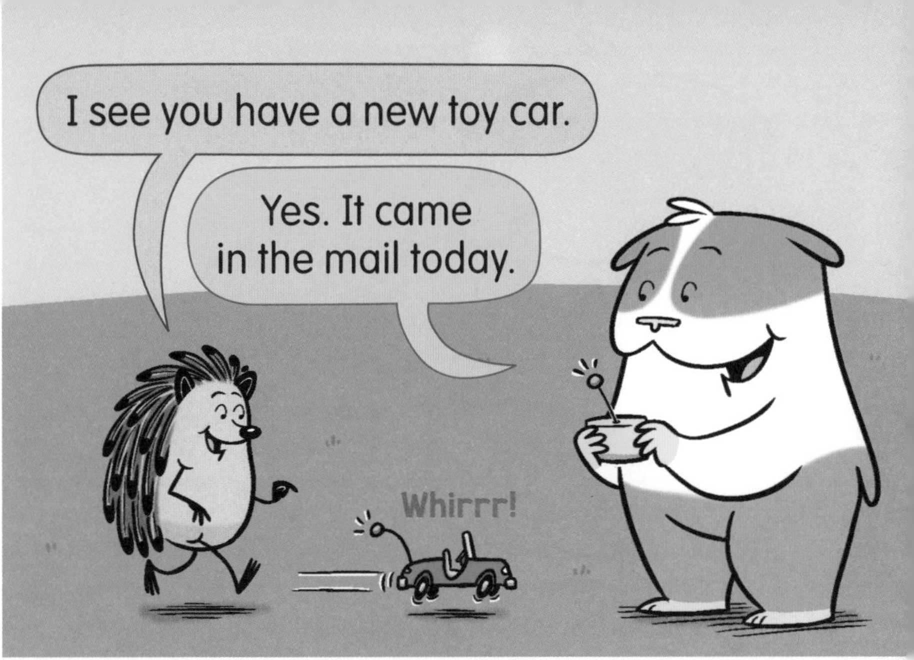
I see you have a new toy car.
Yes. It came in the mail today.
Whirrr!

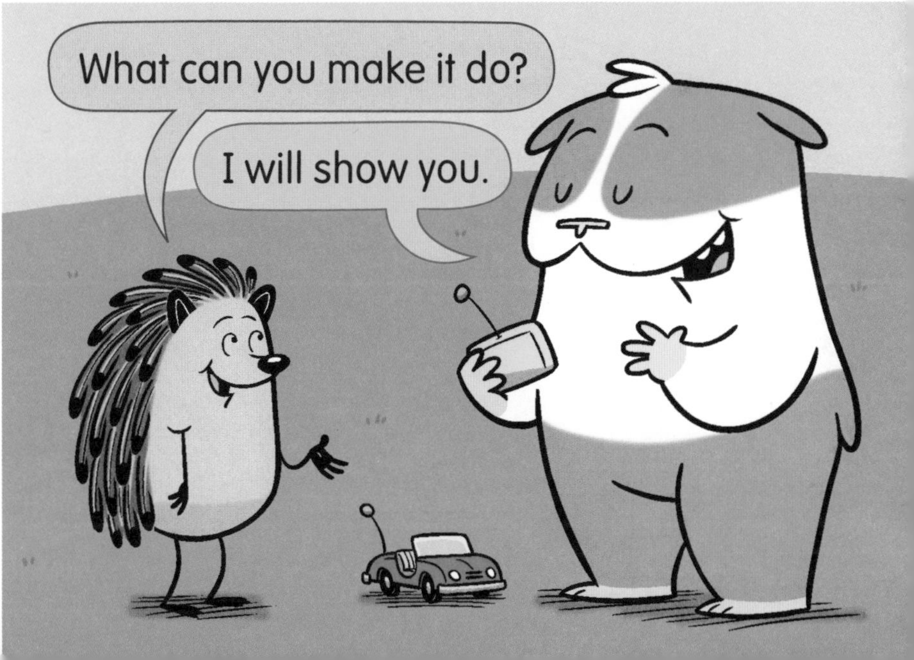
What can you make it do?
I will show you.

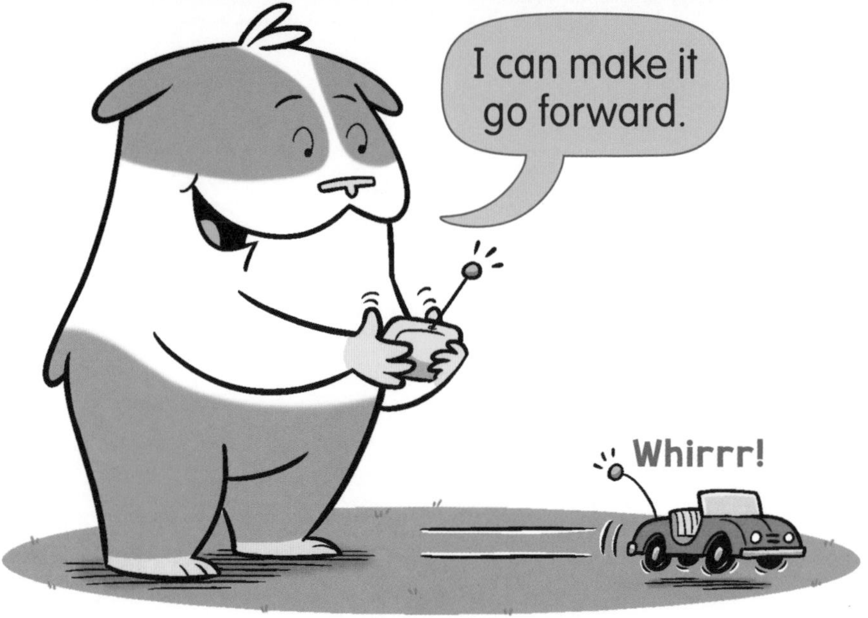
I can make it go forward.
Whirrr!

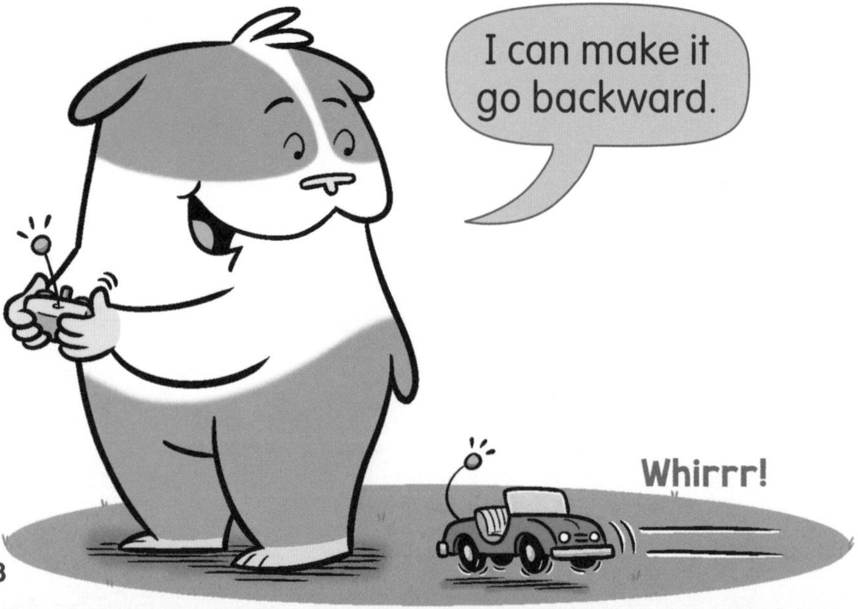
I can make it go backward.
Whirrr!

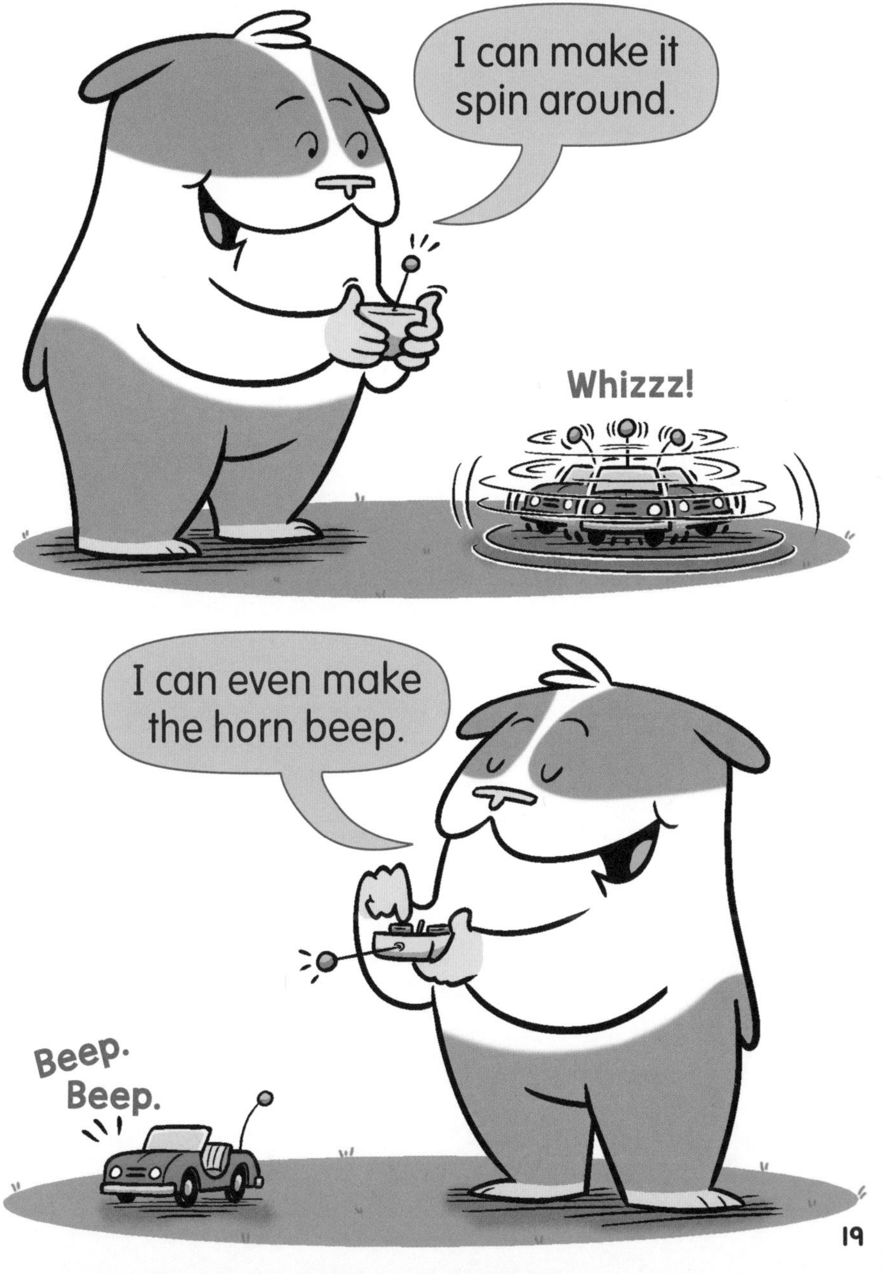
I can make it spin around.
Whizzz!
I can even make the horn beep.
Beep.
Beep.

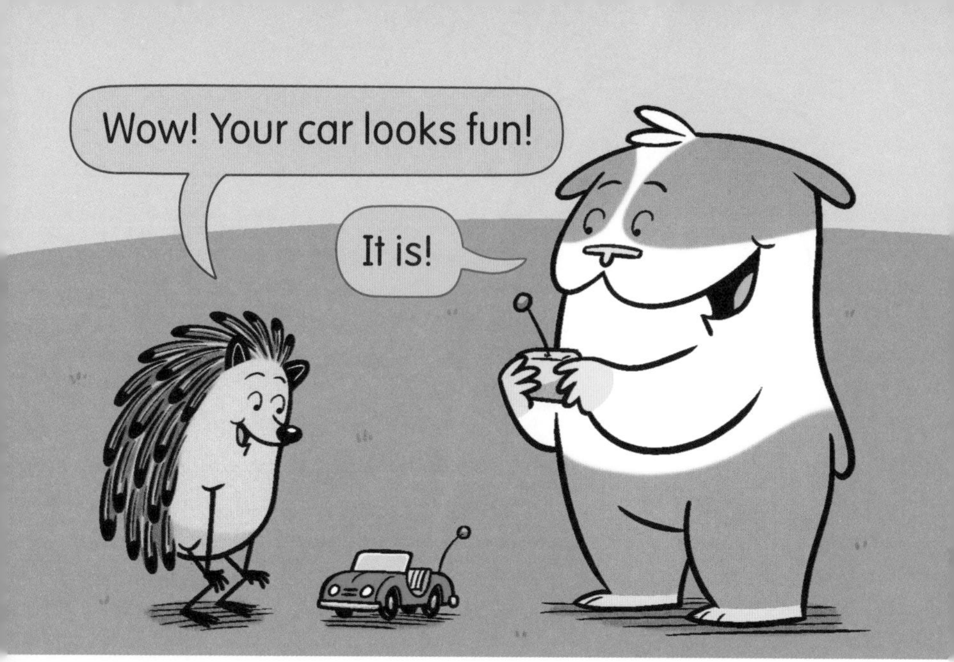
Wow! Your car looks fun!
It is!

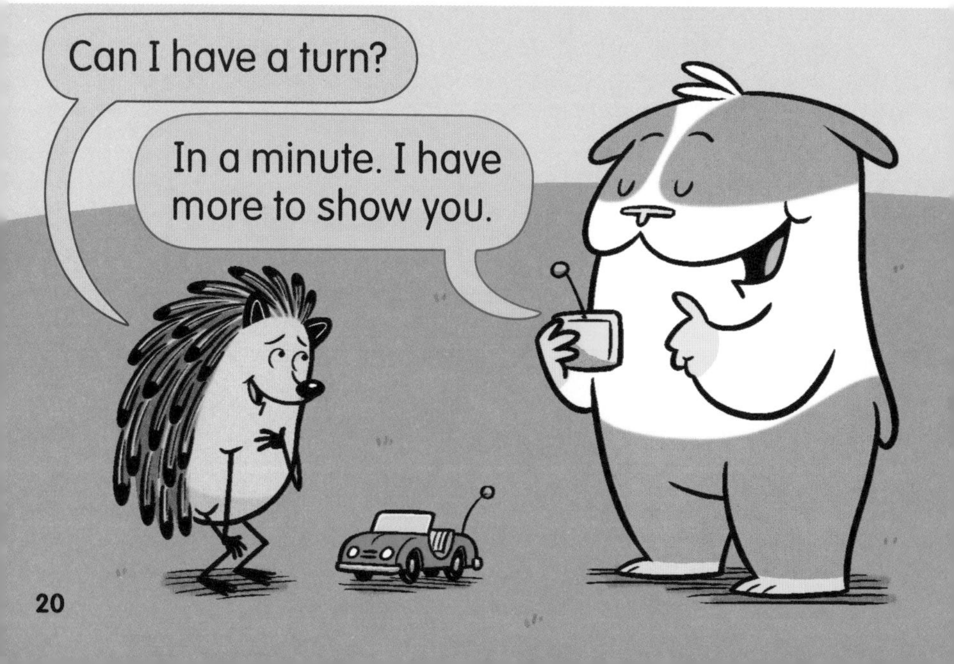
Can I have a turn?
In a minute. I have more to show you.

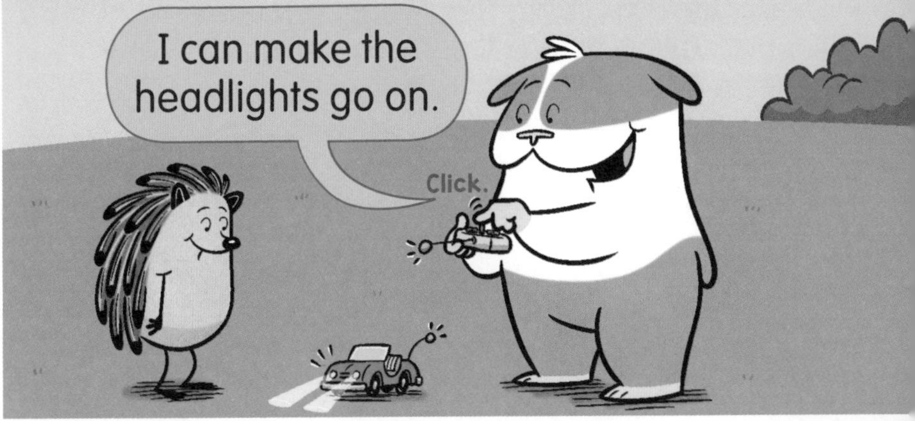
I can make the headlights go on.
Click.

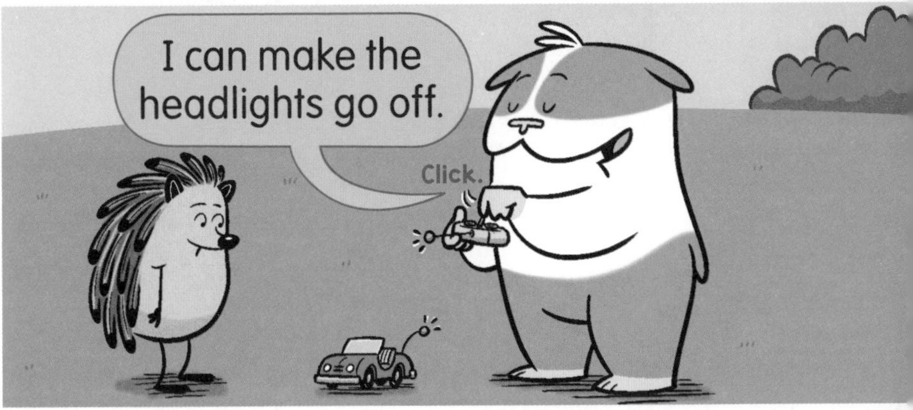
I can make the headlights go off.
Click.

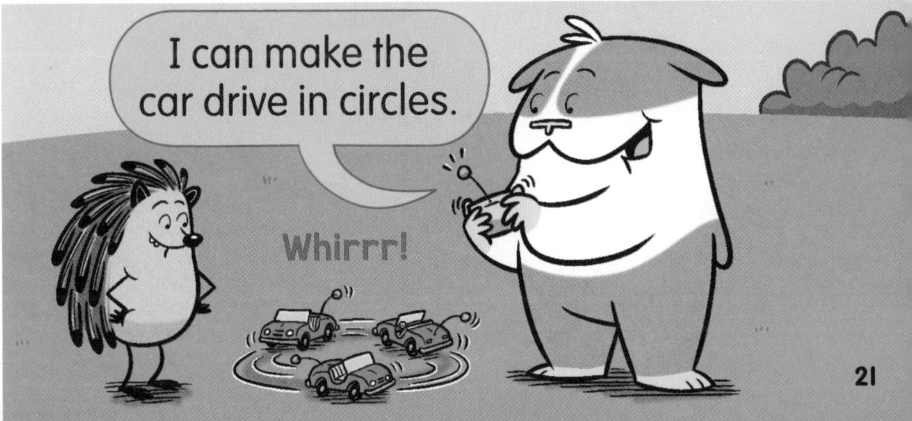
I can make the car drive in circles.
Whirrr!

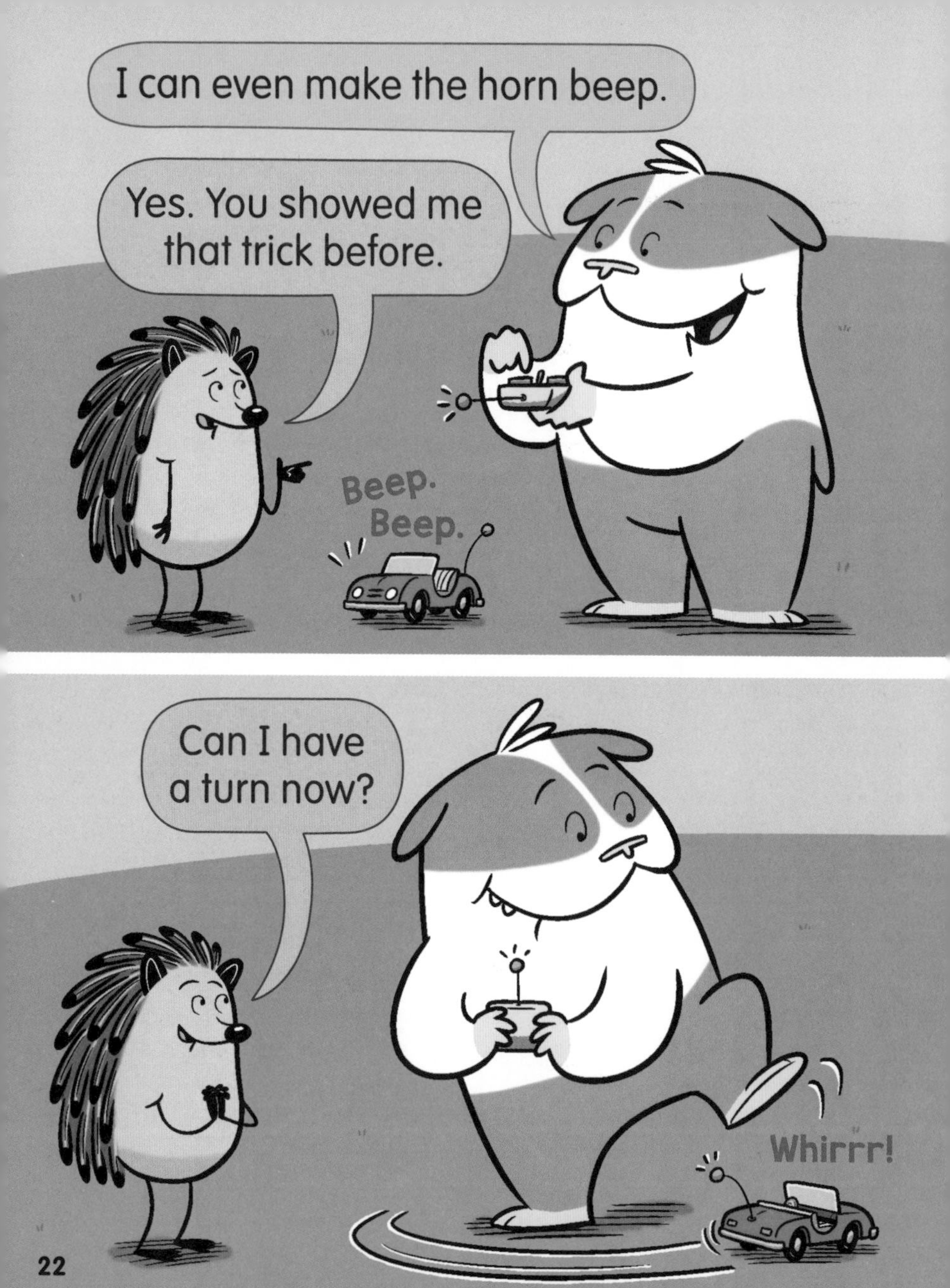
I can even make the horn beep.
Yes. You showed me that trick before.
Beep.
Beep.
Can I have a turn now?
Whirrr!

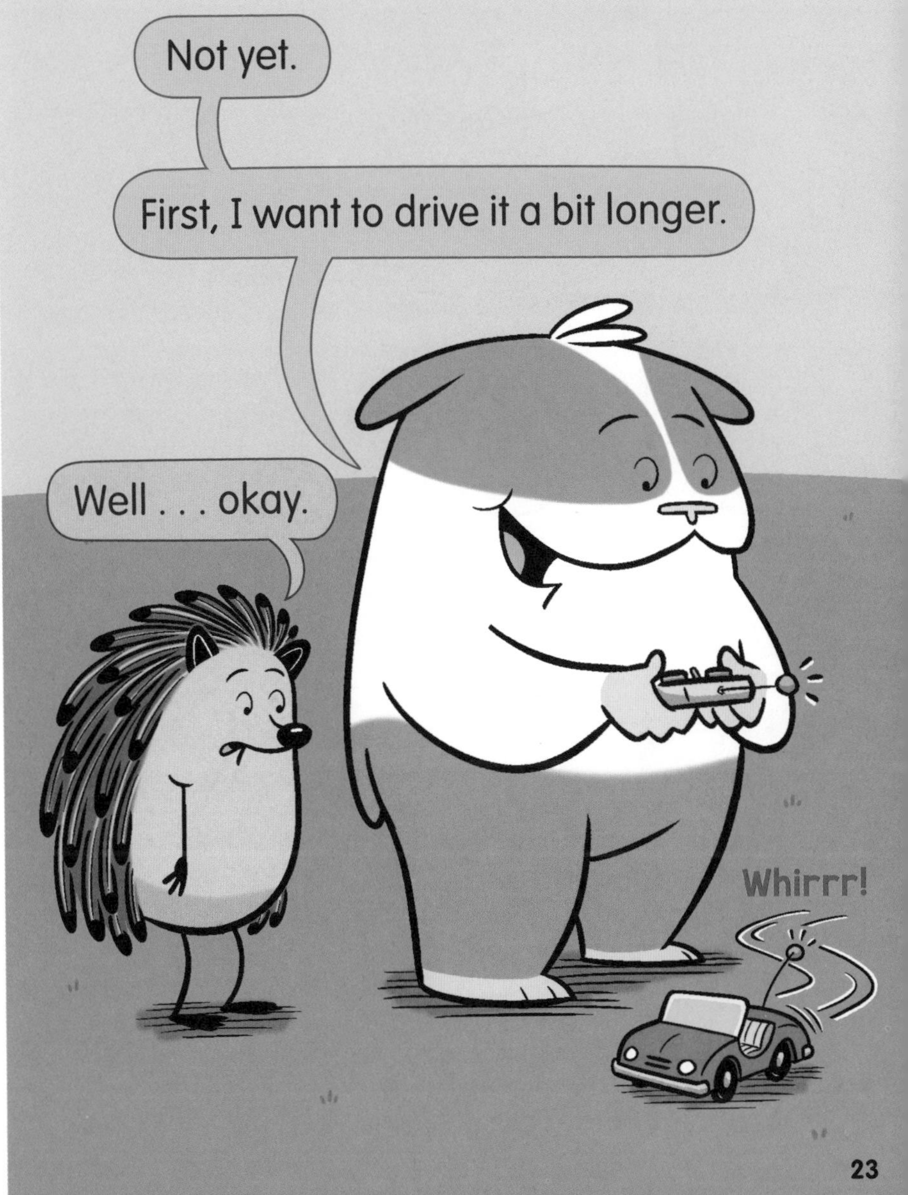
Not yet.
First, I want to drive it a bit longer.
Well . . . okay.
Whirrr!

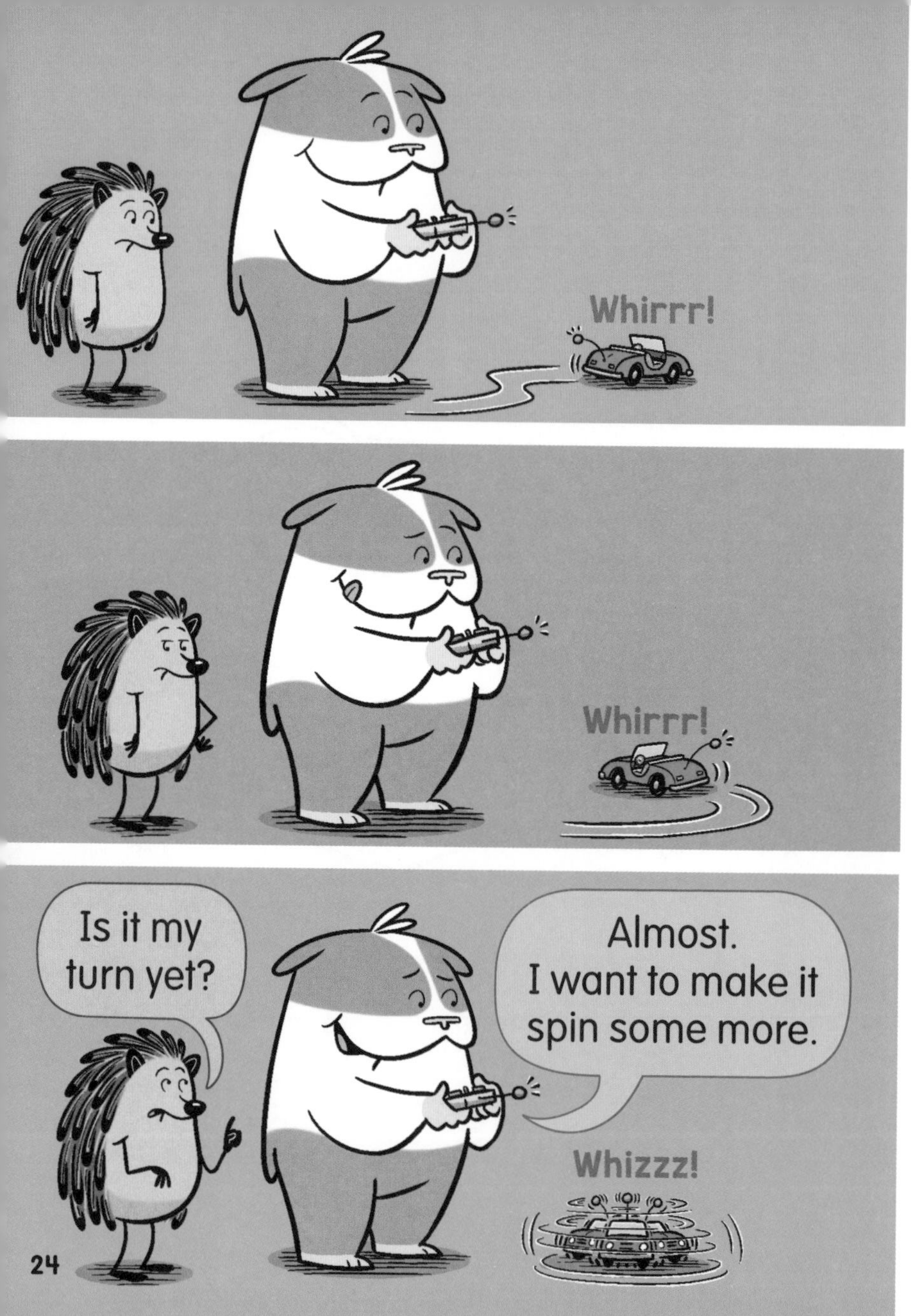
Whirrr!
Whirrr!
Is it my turn yet?
Almost. I want to make it spin some more.
Whizzz!

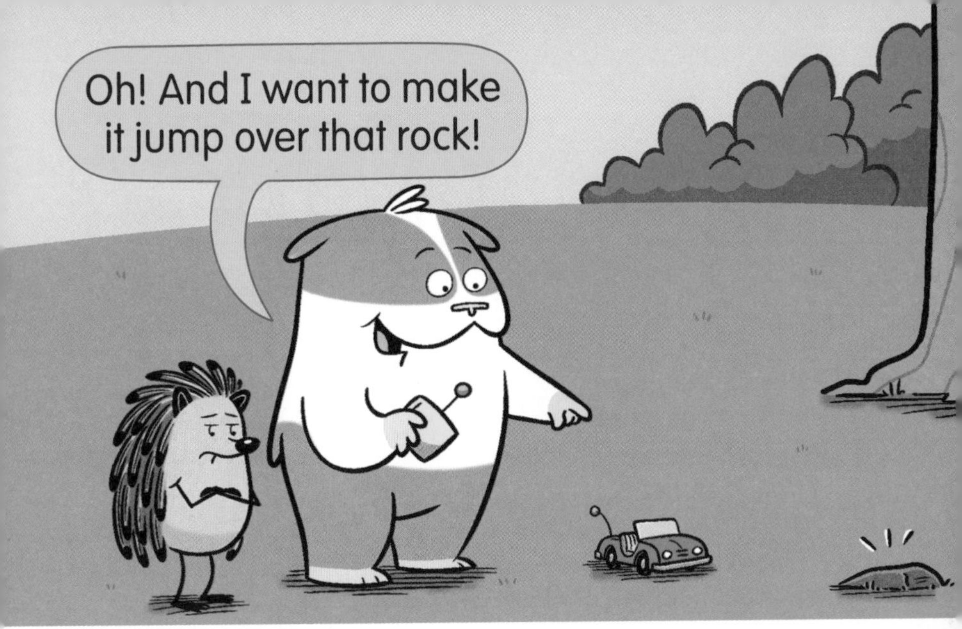
Oh! And I want to make it jump over that rock!

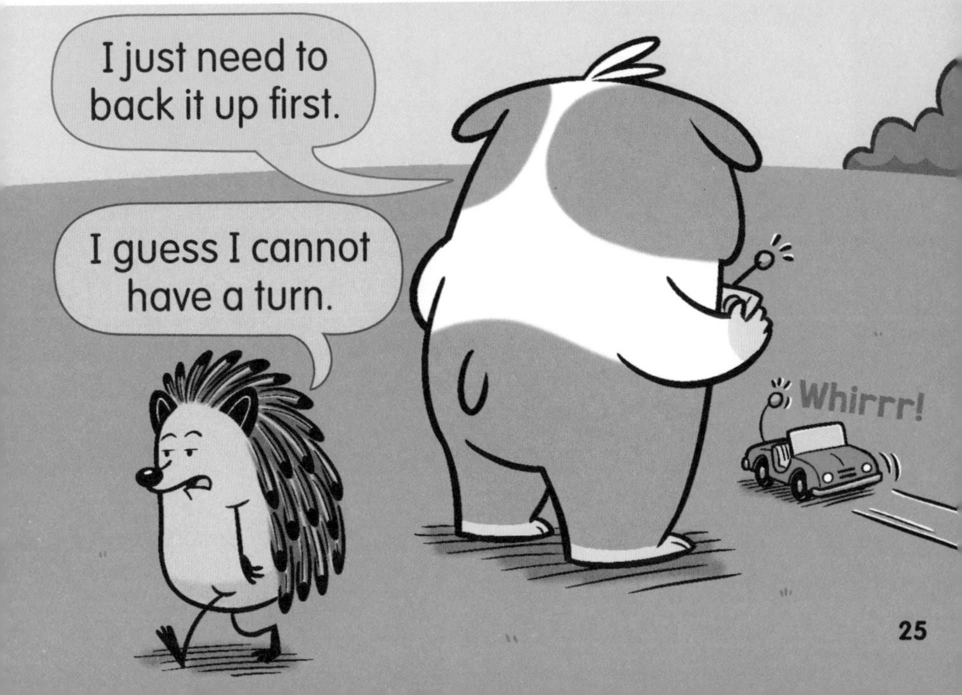
I just need to back it up first.
I guess I cannot have a turn.
Whirrr!

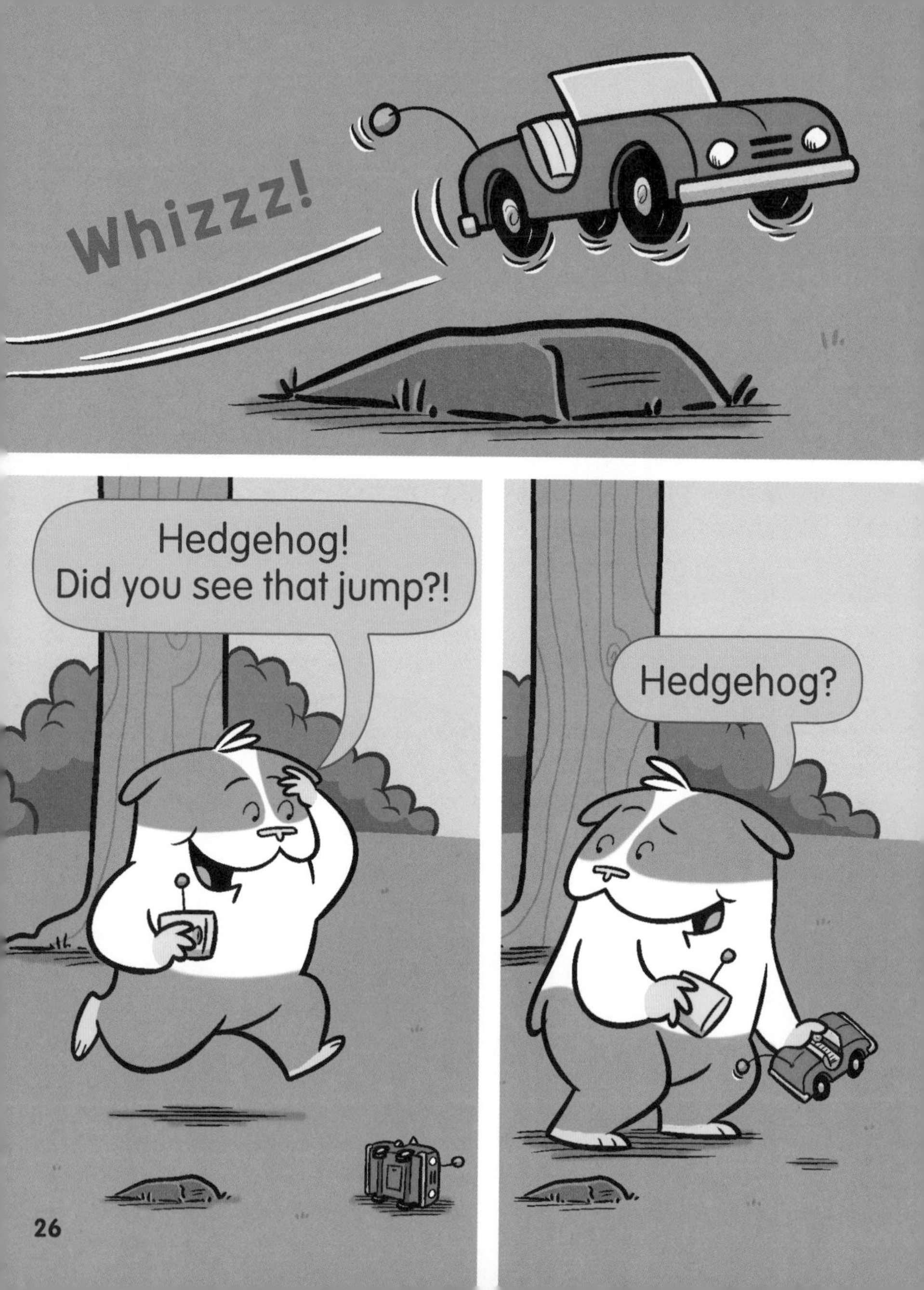
Whizzzz!
Hedgehog! Did you see that jump?!
Hedgehog?

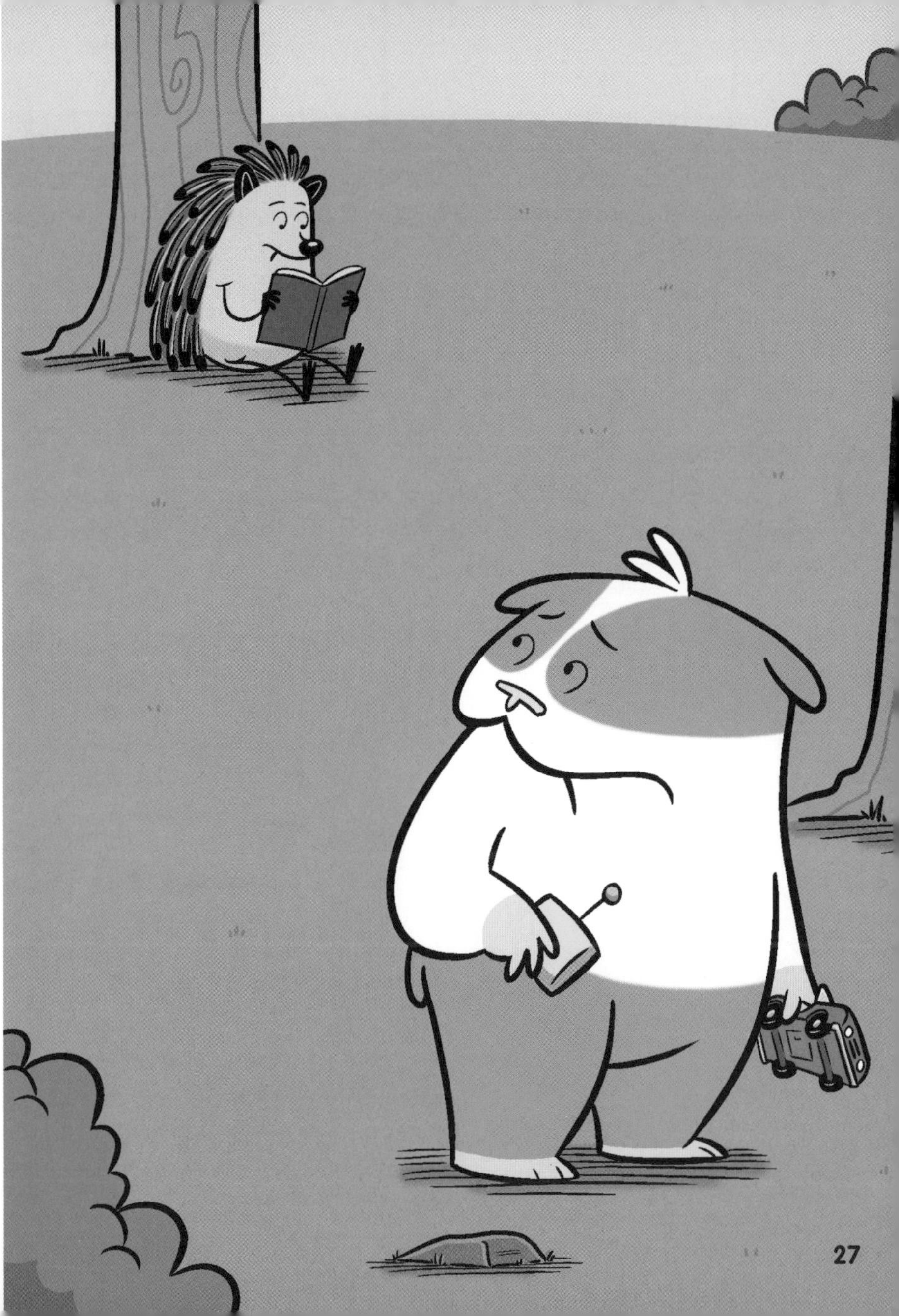

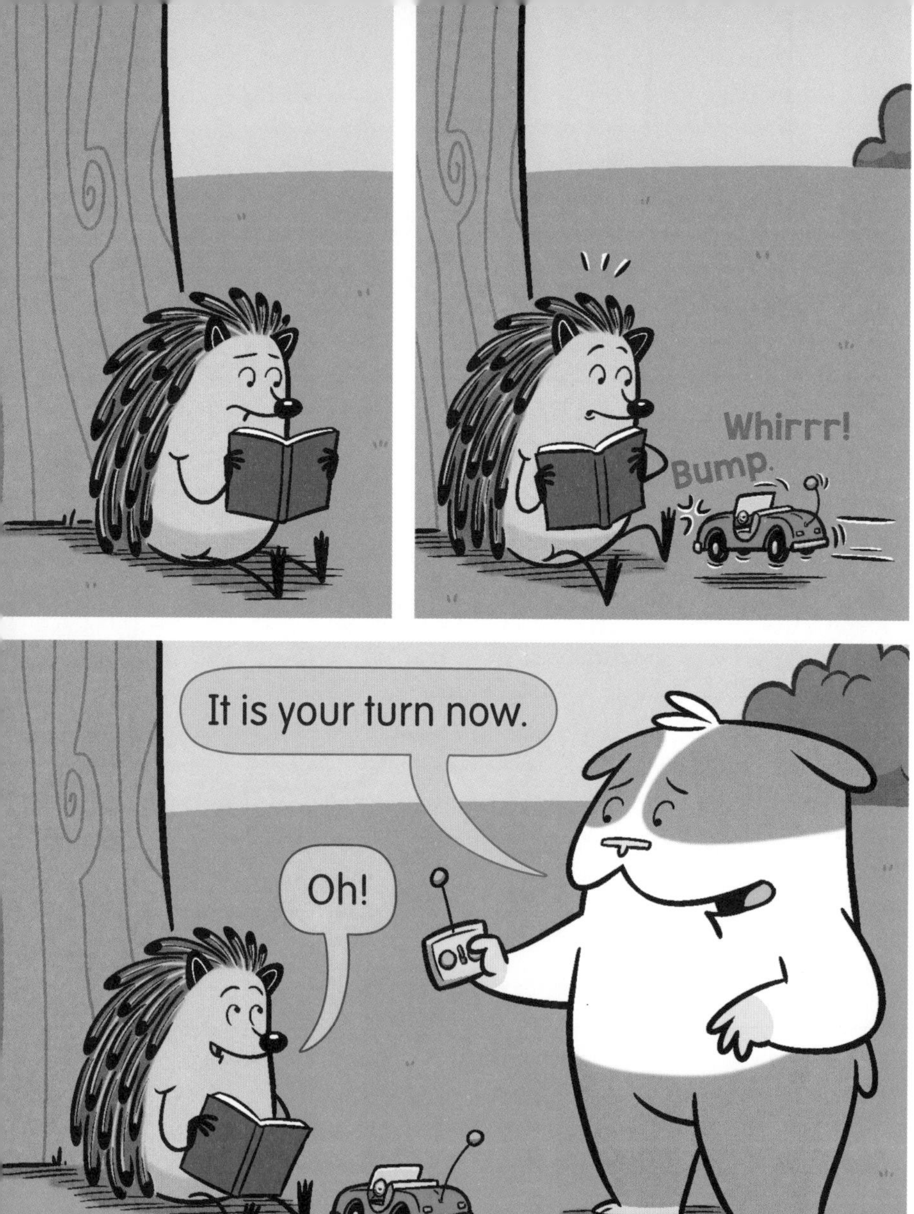
Whirrr!
Bump.
It is your turn now.
Oh!

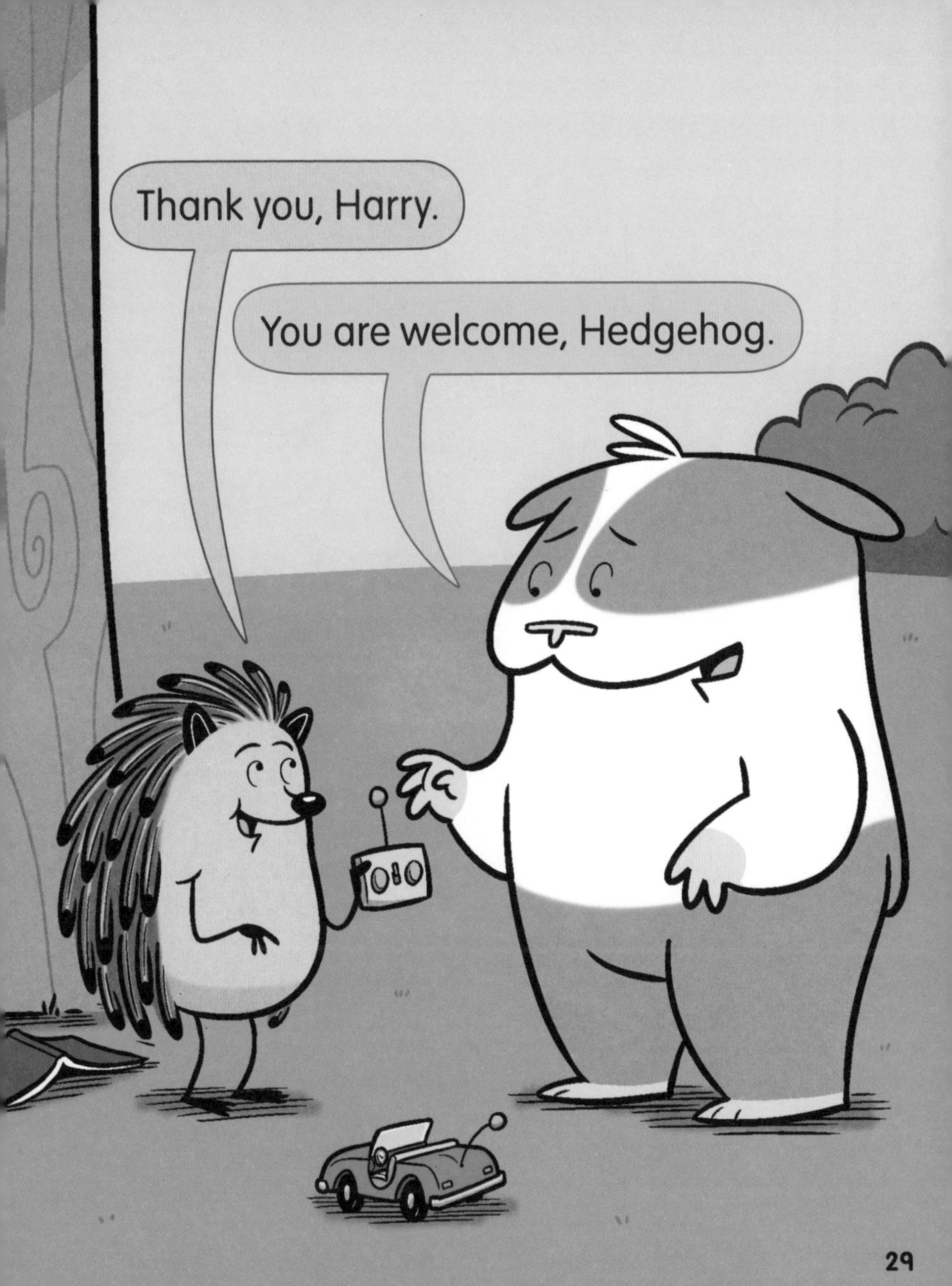
Thank you, Harry.
You are welcome, Hedgehog.

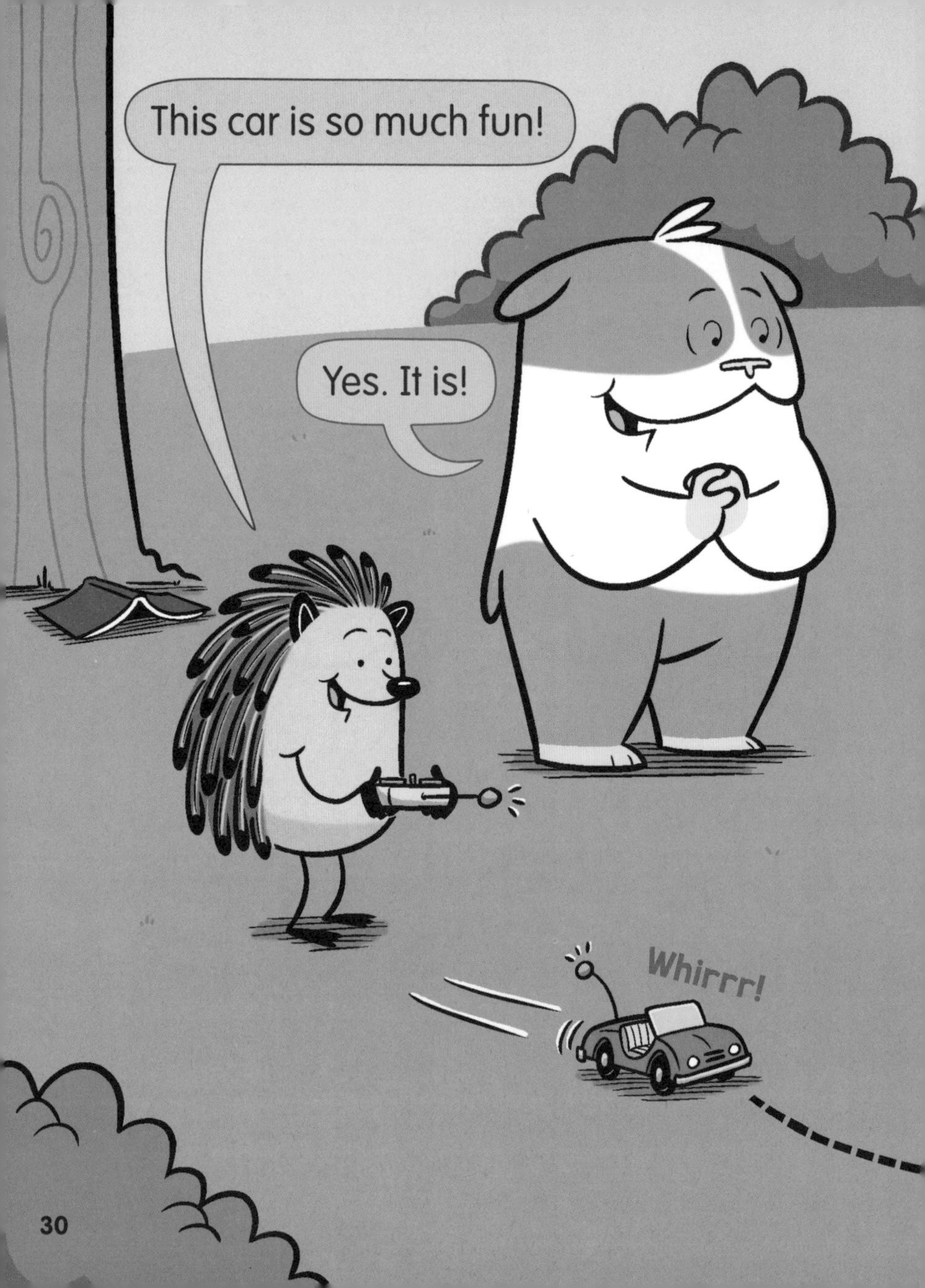
This car is so much fun!
Yes. It is!
Whirrr!

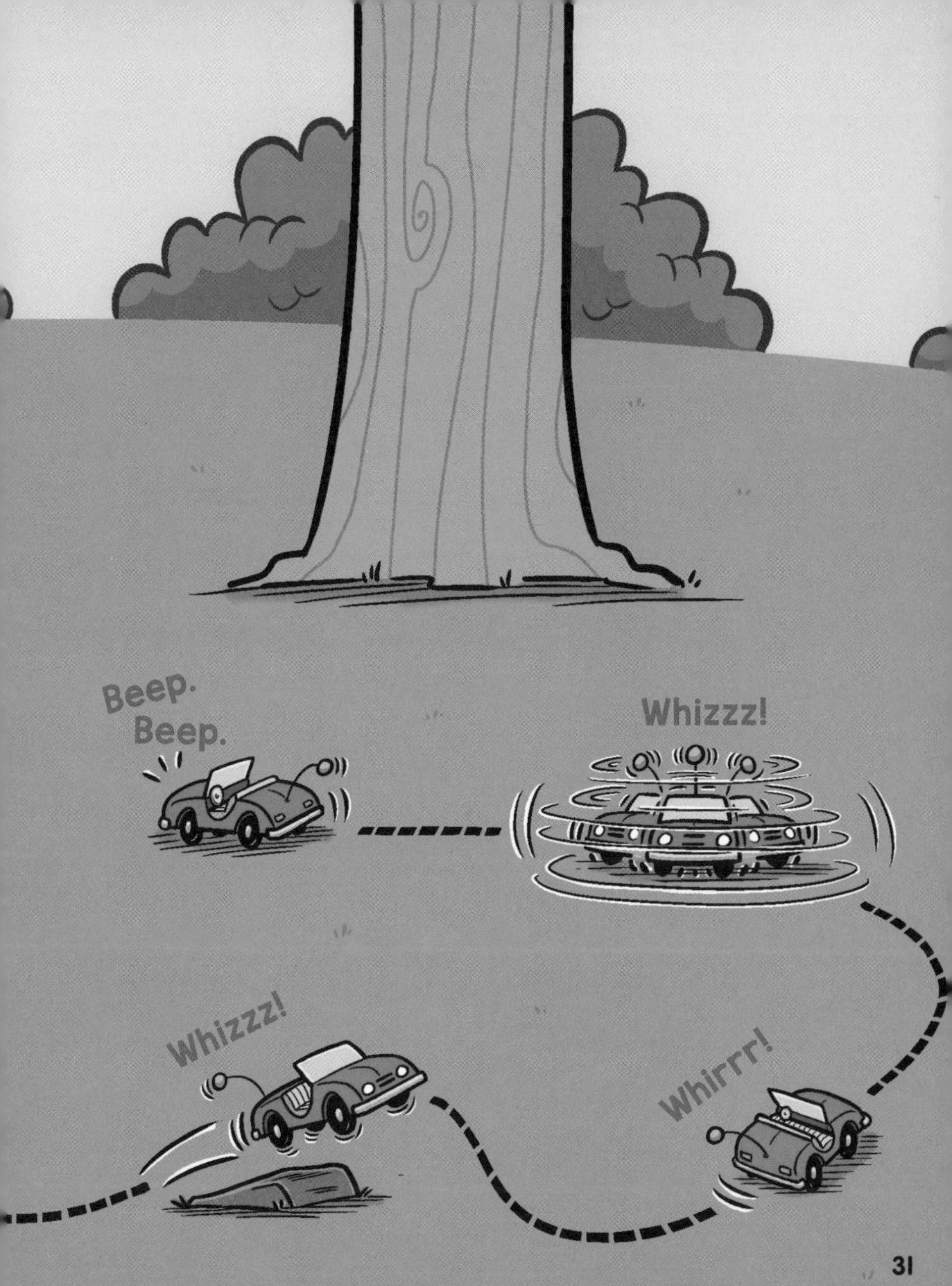
Beep.
Beep.
Whizzz!
Whizzz!
Whirrr!

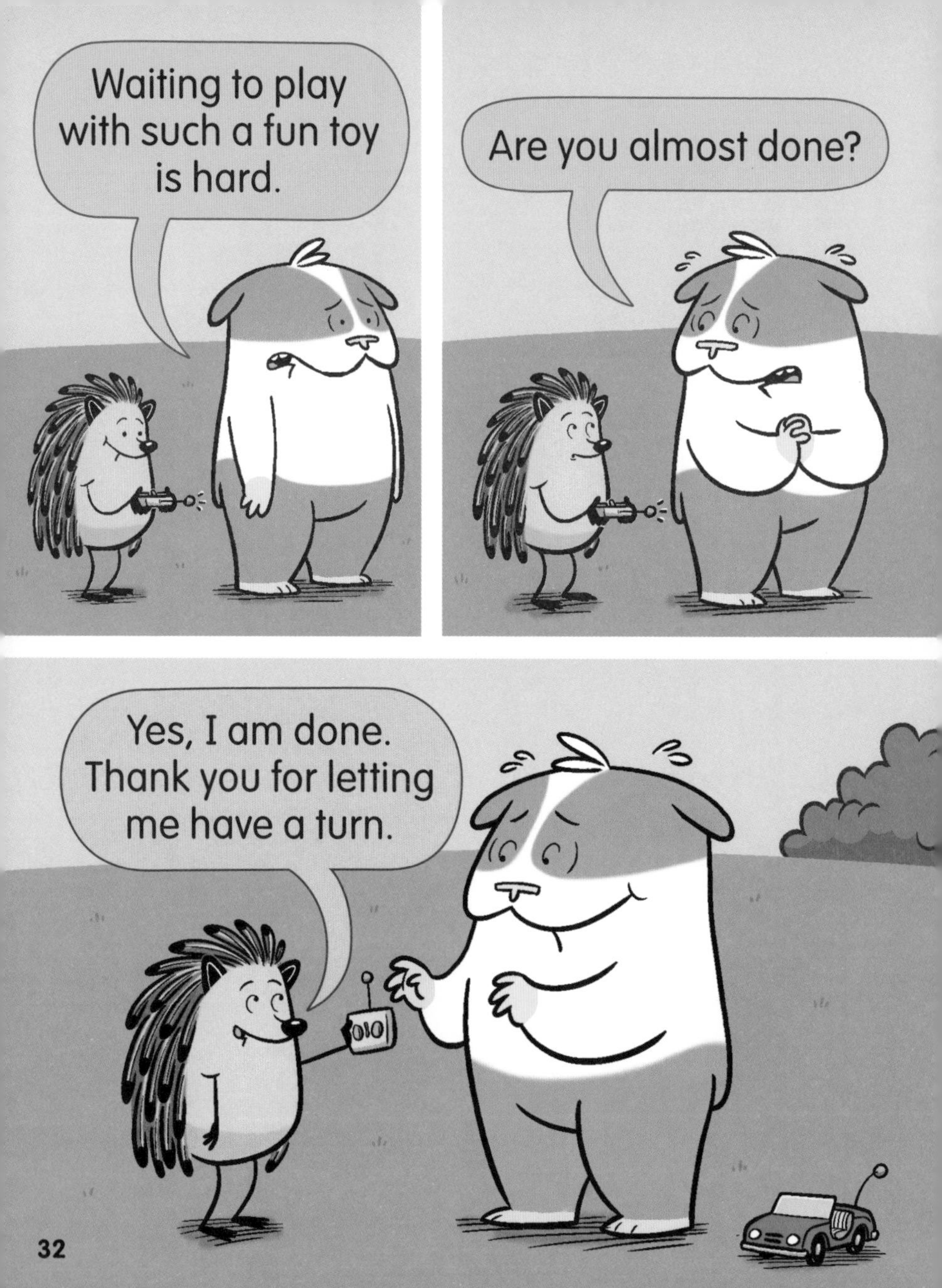
Waiting to play with such a fun toy is hard.
Are you almost done?
Yes, I am done. Thank you for letting me have a turn.

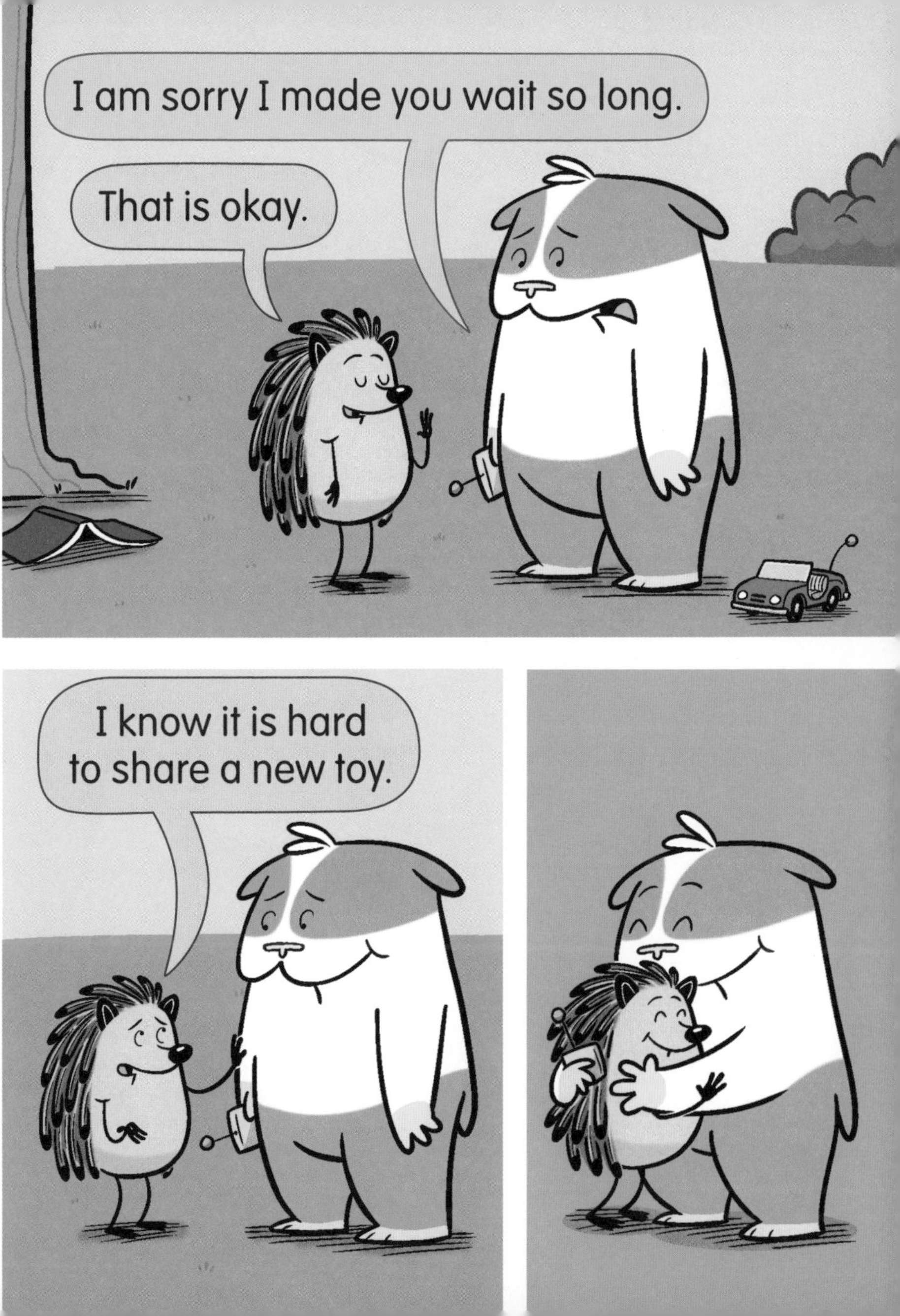
I am sorry I made you wait so long.
That is okay.
I know it is hard
to share a new toy.

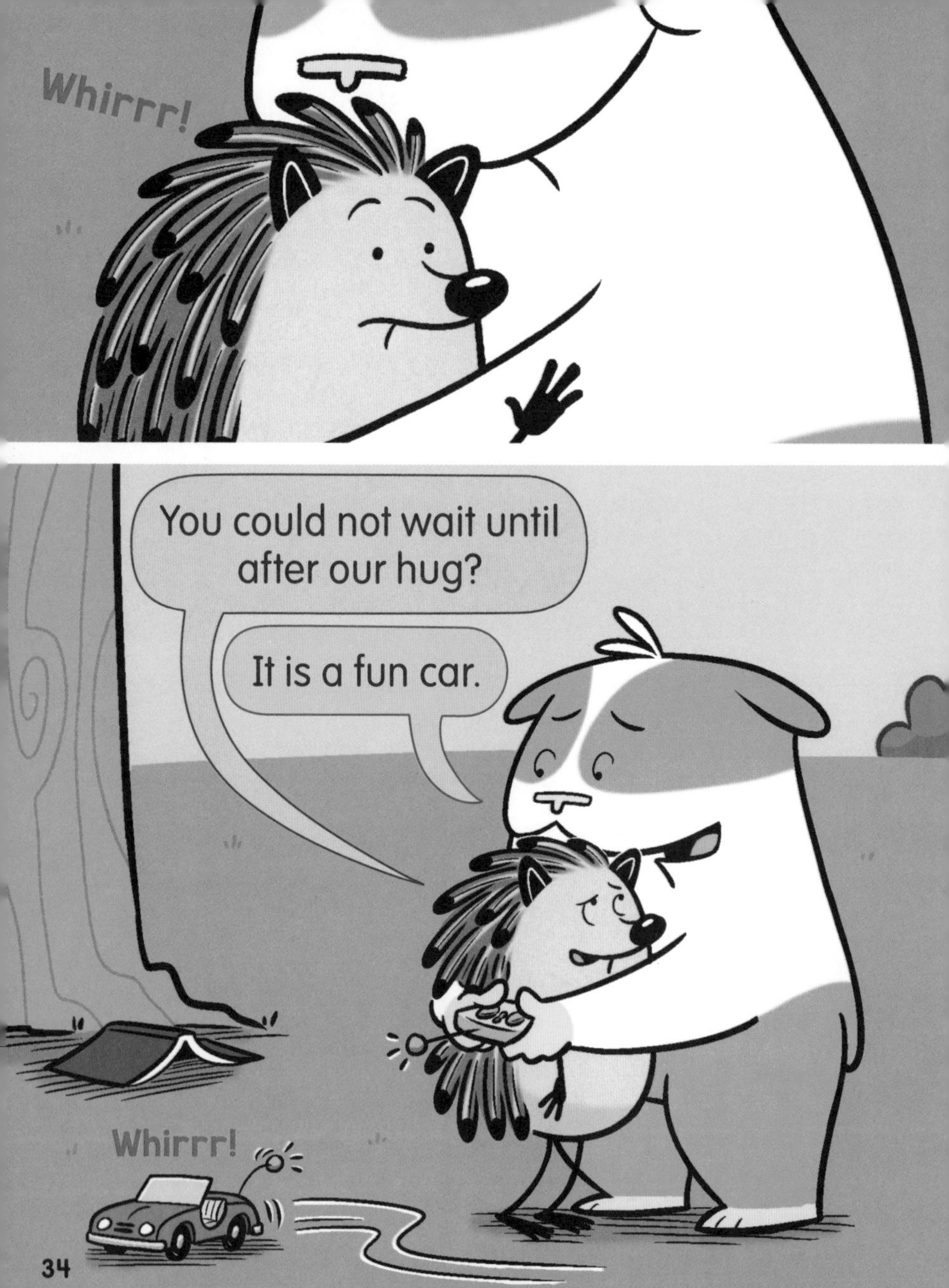
Whirrr!
You could not wait until after our hug?
It is a fun car.
Whirrr!

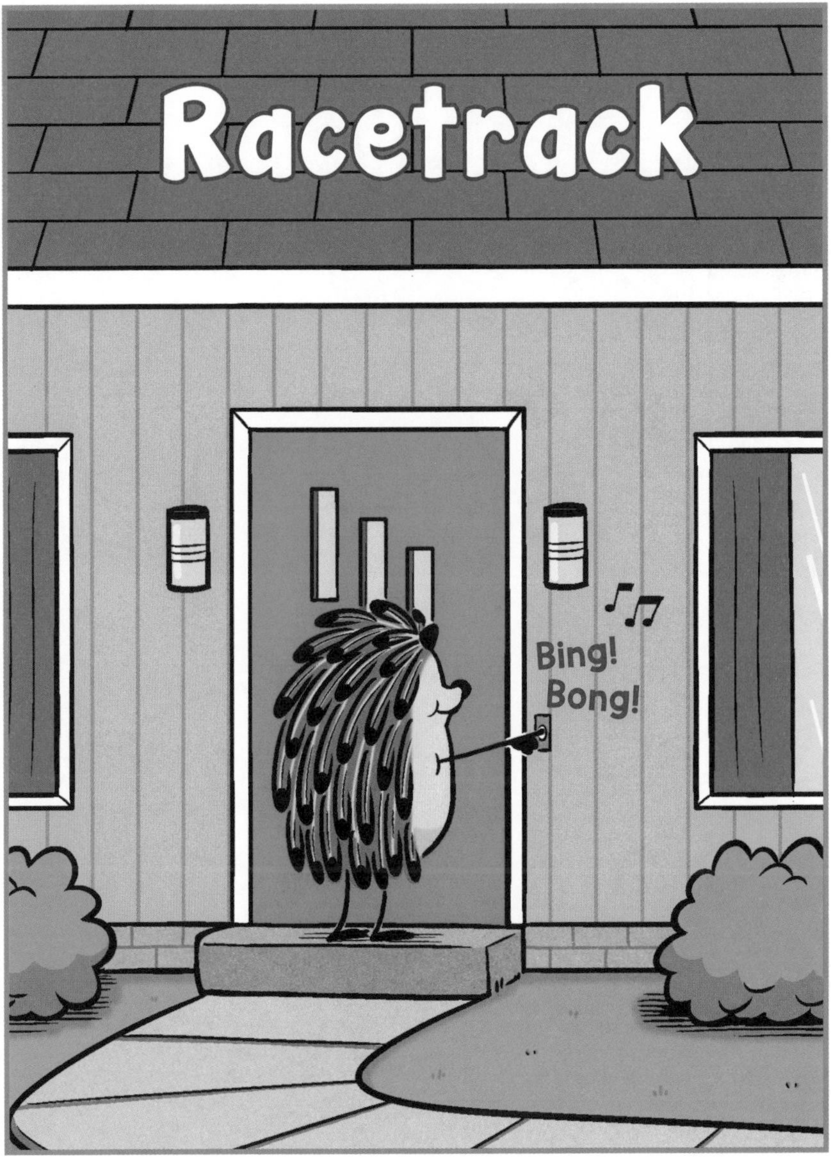
Racetrack
Bing! Bong!

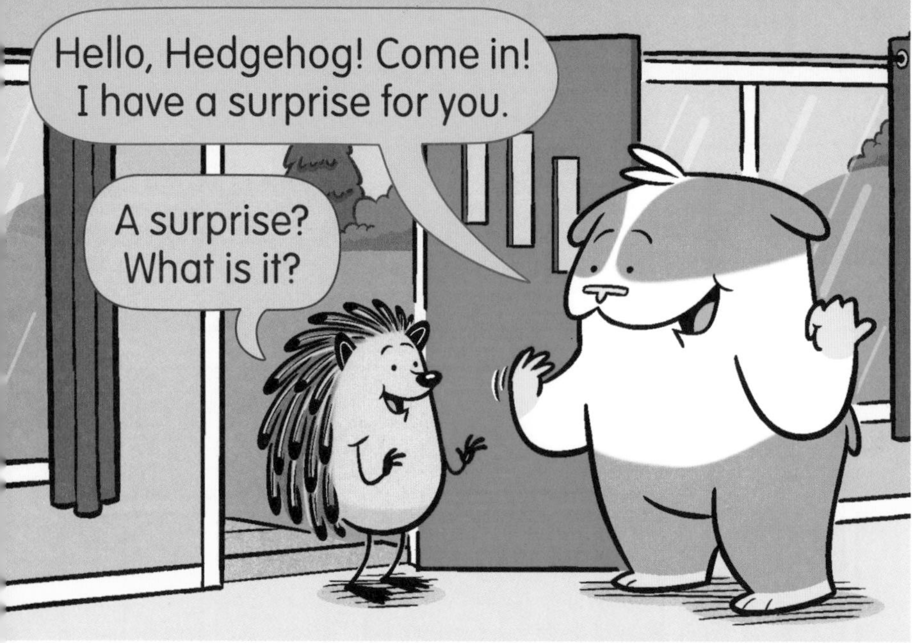
Hello, Hedgehog! Come in!
I have a surprise for you.
A surprise?
What is it?

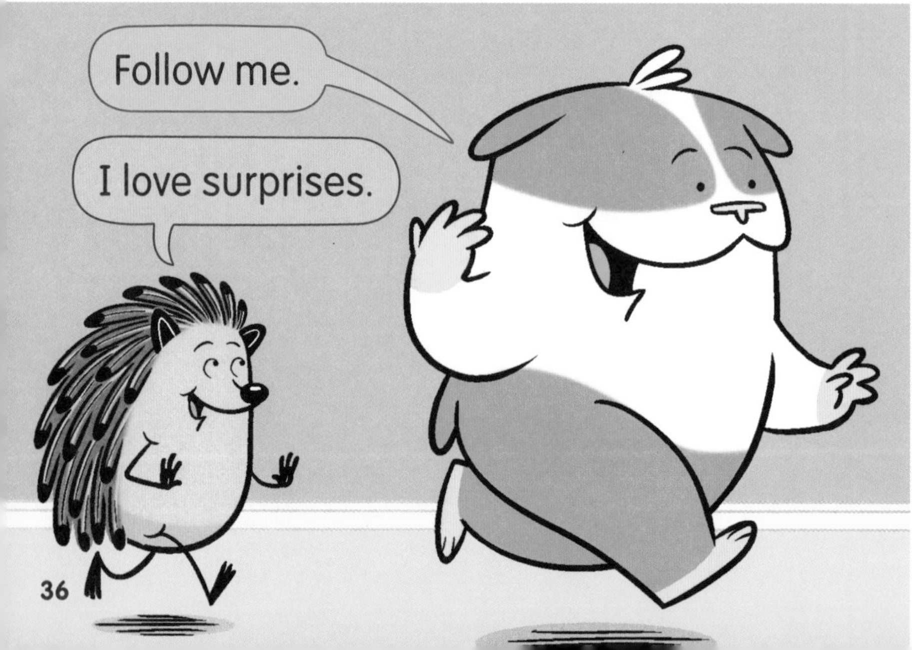
Follow me.
I love surprises.

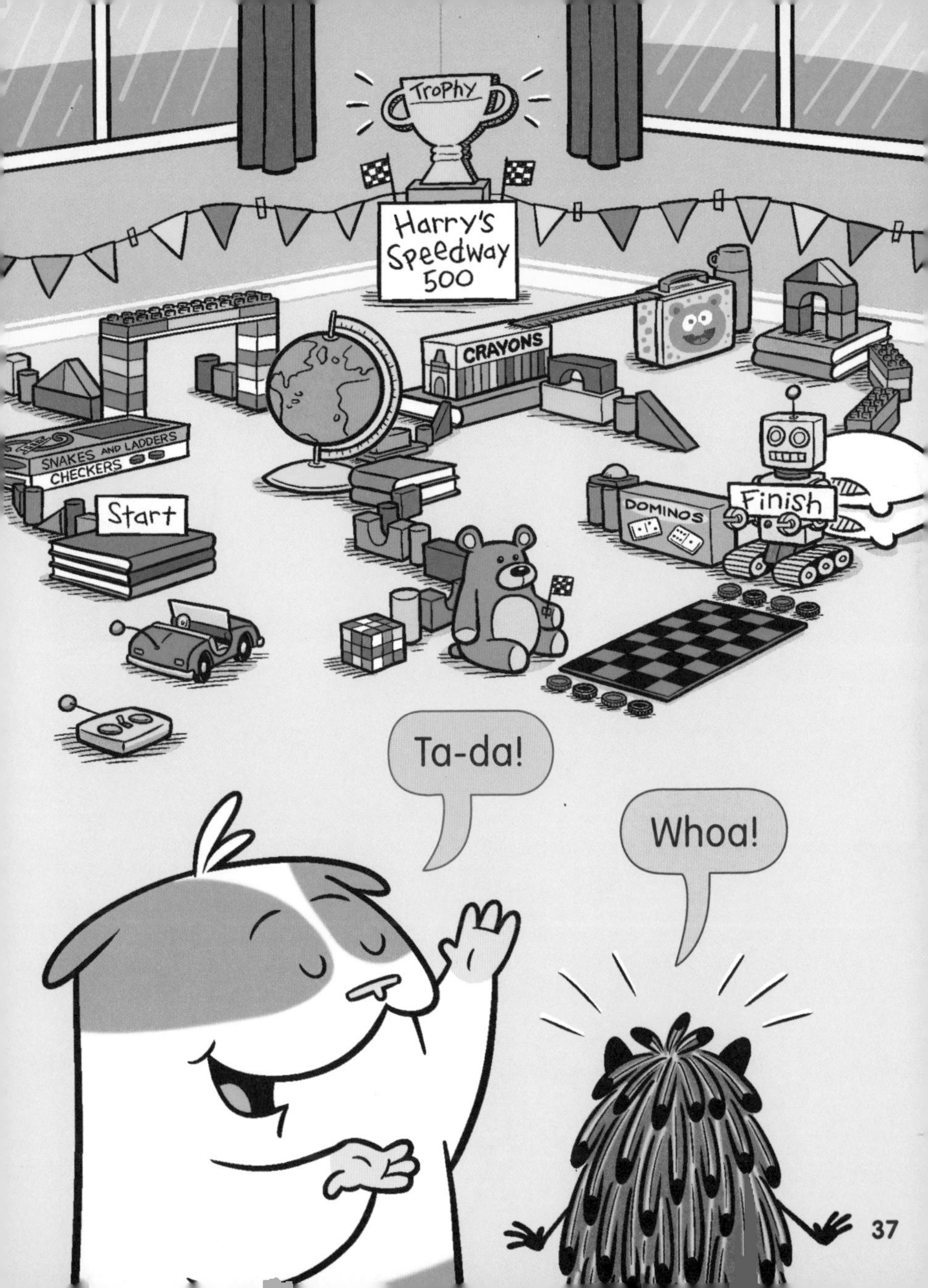
Trophy
Harry's Speedway 500
CRAYONS
SNAKES AND LADDERS
CHECKERS
Start
DOMINOS
Finish
Ta-da!
Whoa!

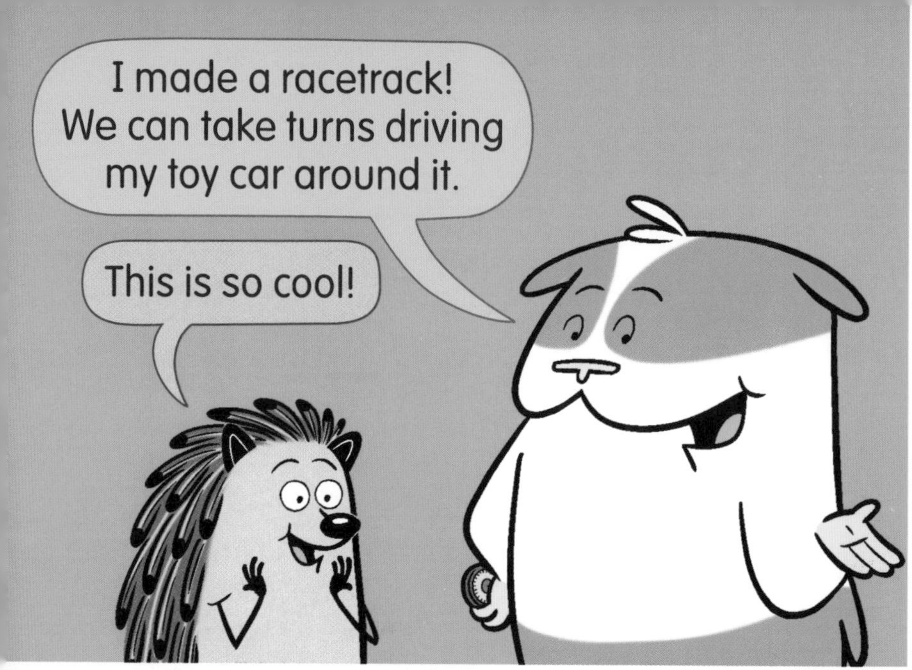
I made a racetrack! We can take turns driving my toy car around it.
This is so cool!

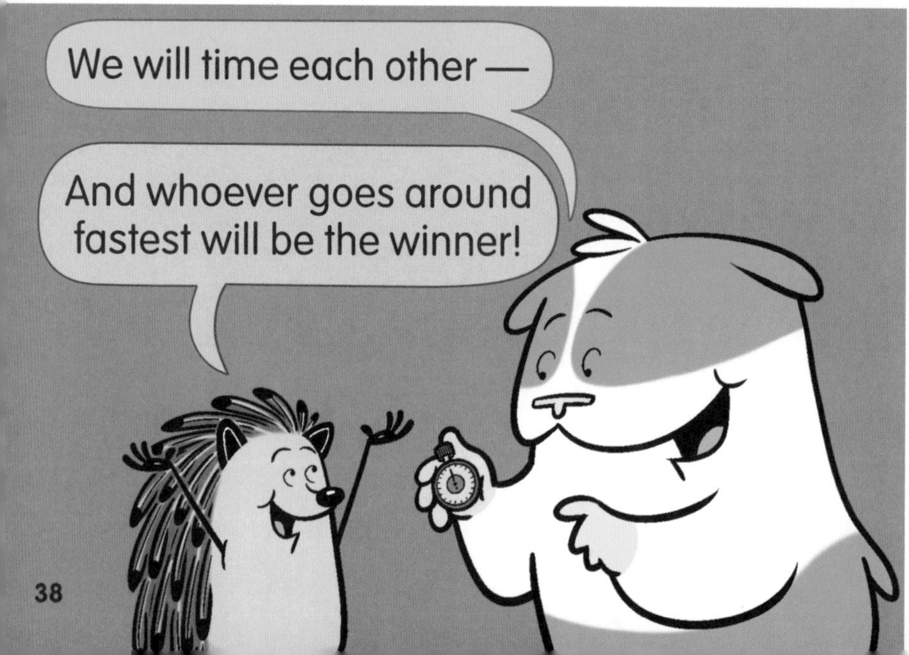
We will time each other —
And whoever goes around fastest will be the winner!

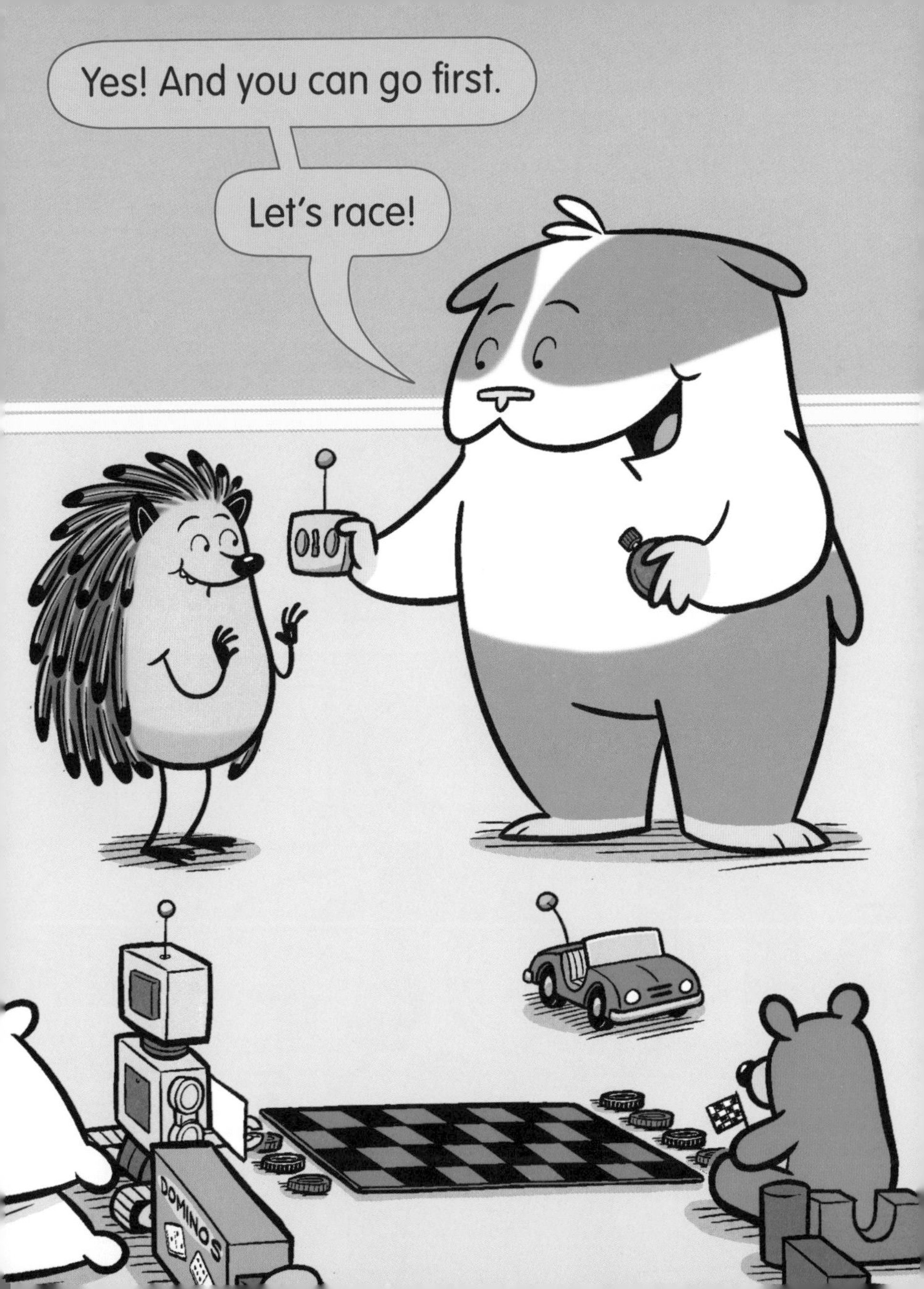
Let's race!
Yes! And you can go first.
DOMINOS

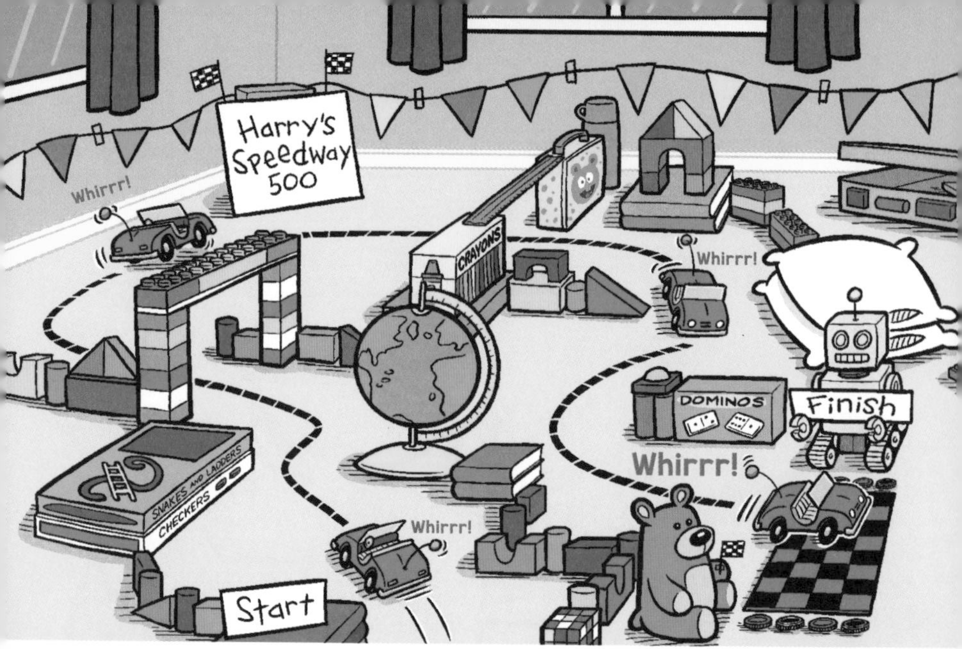
Harry's Speedway 500
Whirrr!
CRAYONS
Whirrr!
DOMINOS
Finish
Whirrr!
SNAKES AND LADDERS
CHECKERS
Whirrr!
Start

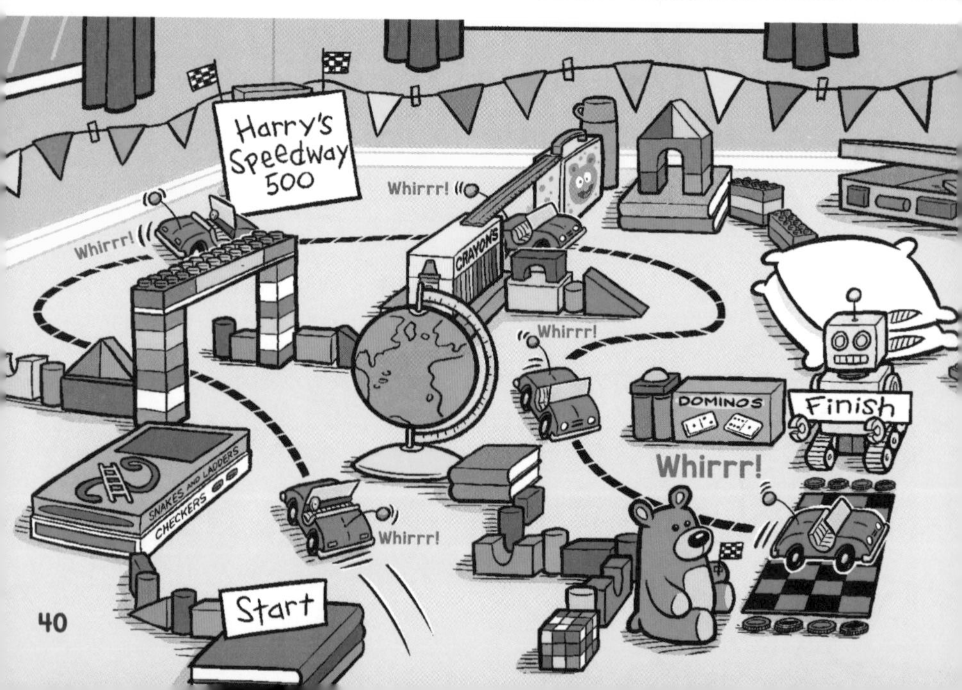
Harry's Speedway 500
Whirrr!
Whirrr!
CRAYONS
Whirrr!
DOMINOS
Finish
Whirrr!
SNAKES AND LADDERS
CHECKERS
Whirrr!
Start

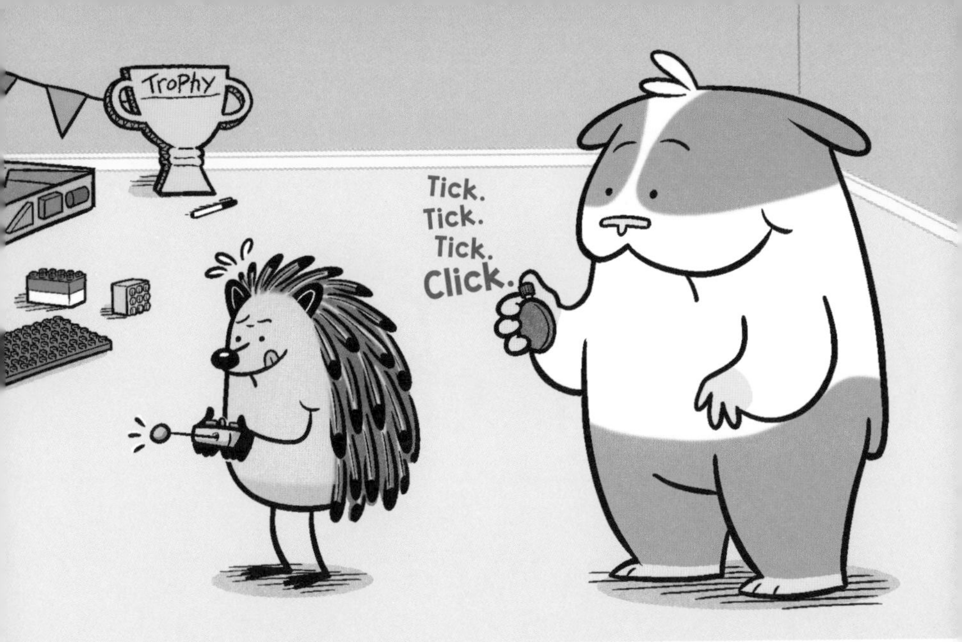
TROPHY
Tick.
Tick.
Tick.
Click.

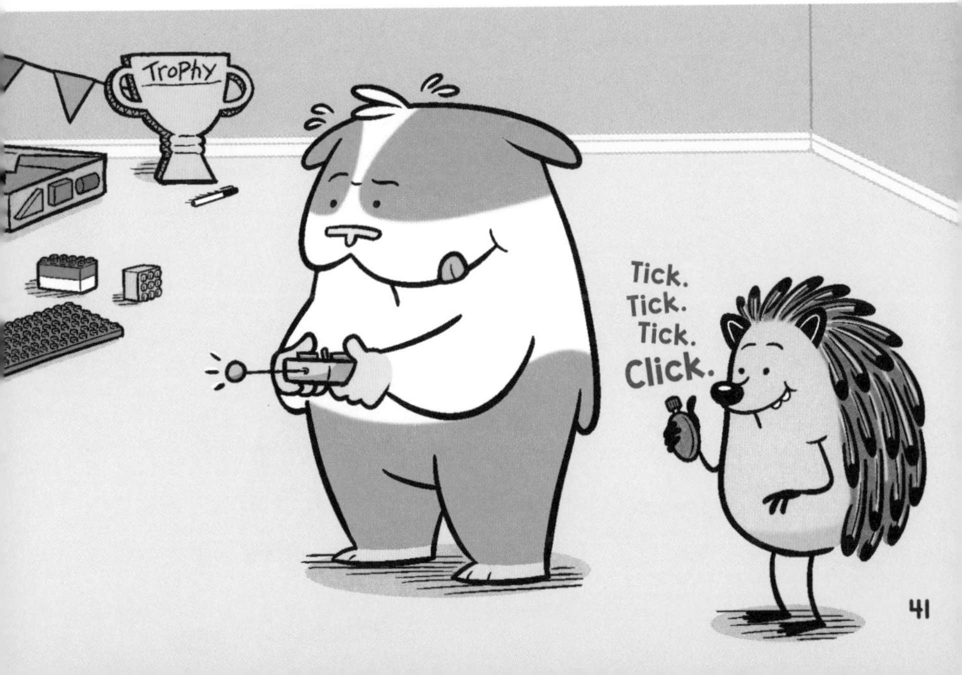
TROPHY
Tick.
Tick.
Tick.
Click.

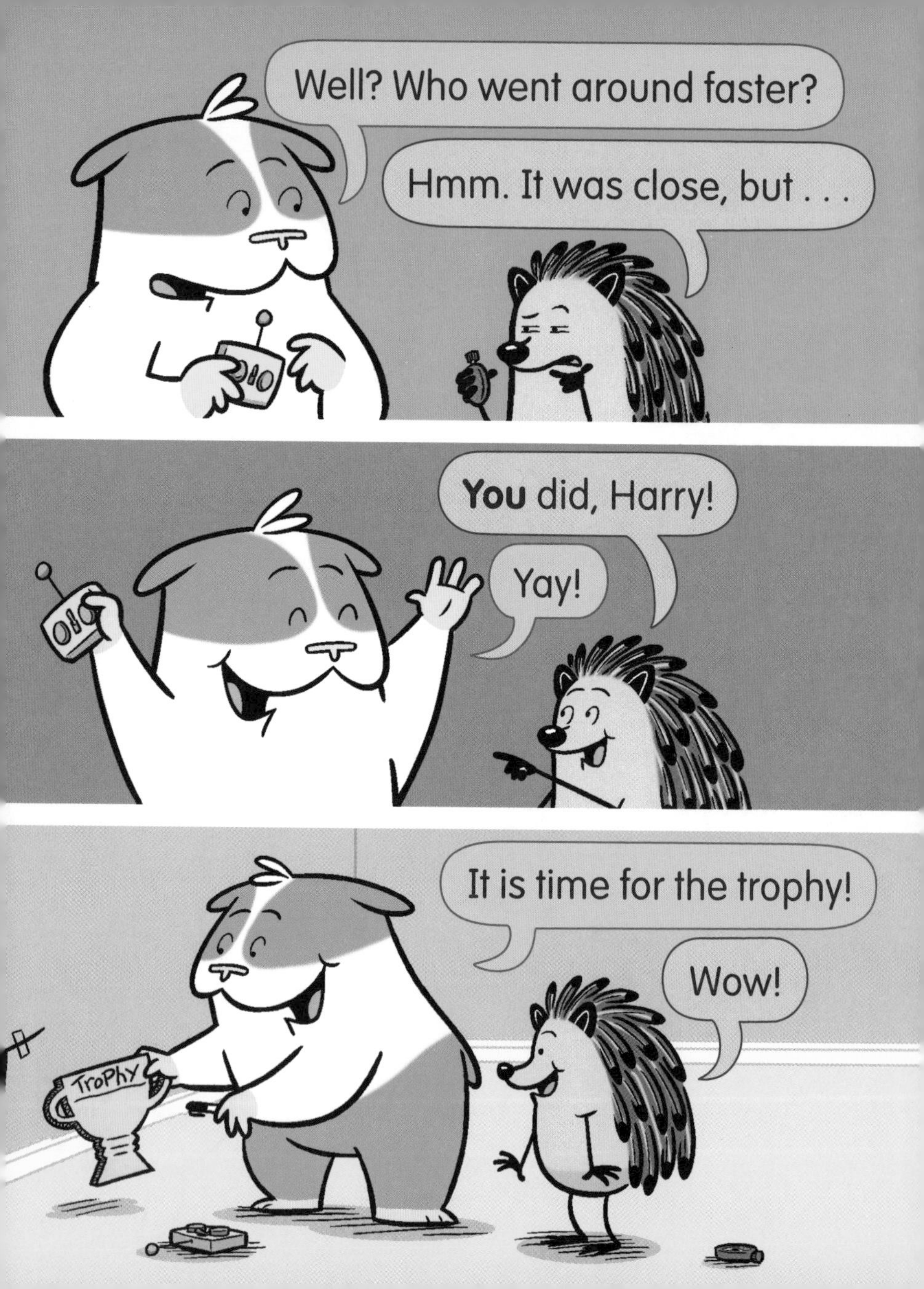
Well? Who went around faster?
Hmm. It was close, but . . .
You did, Harry!
Yay!
It is time for the trophy!
Wow!
TroPhy

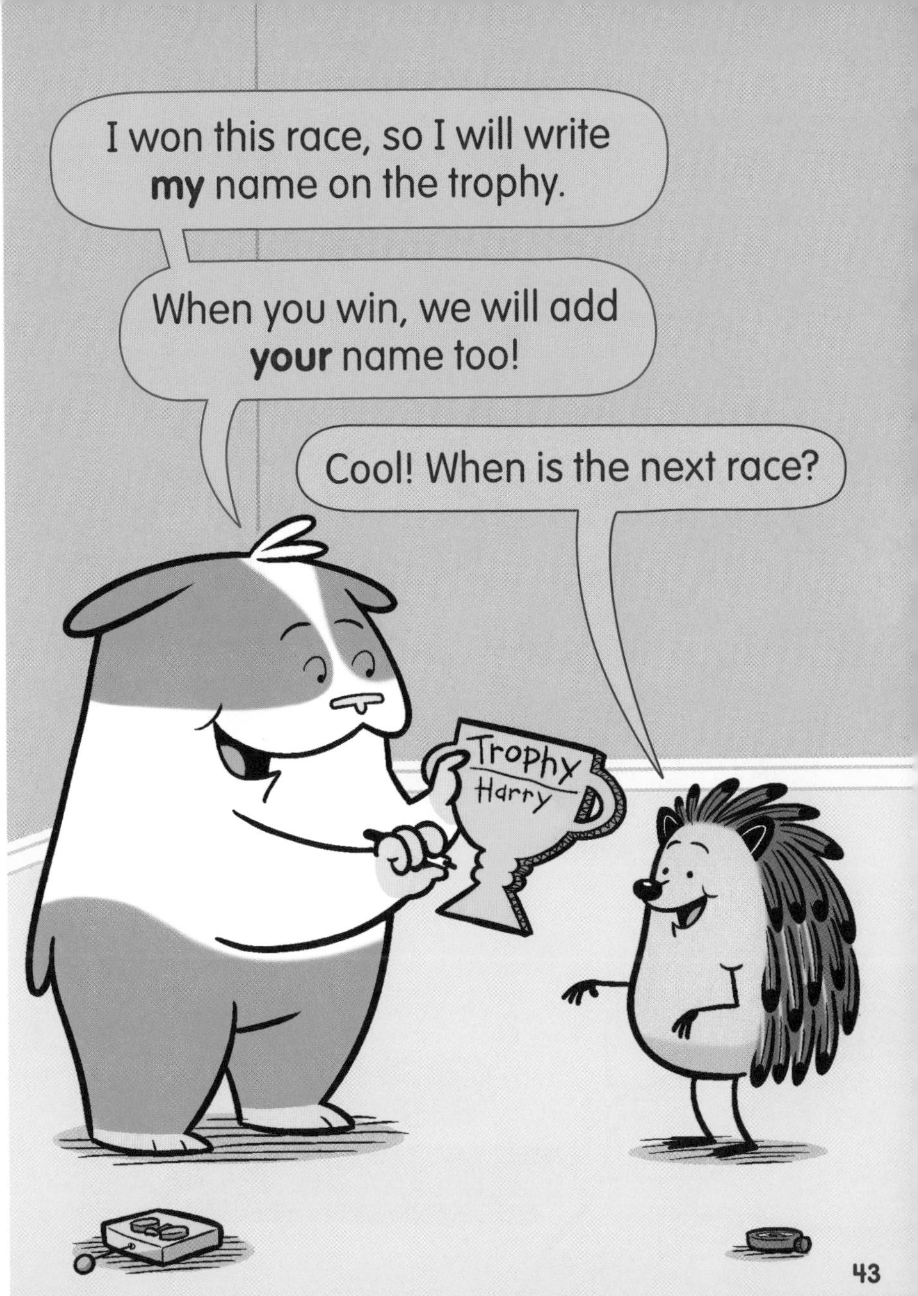
I won this race, so I will write **my** name on the trophy.
When you win, we will add **your** name too!
Cool! When is the next race?
Trophy
Harry

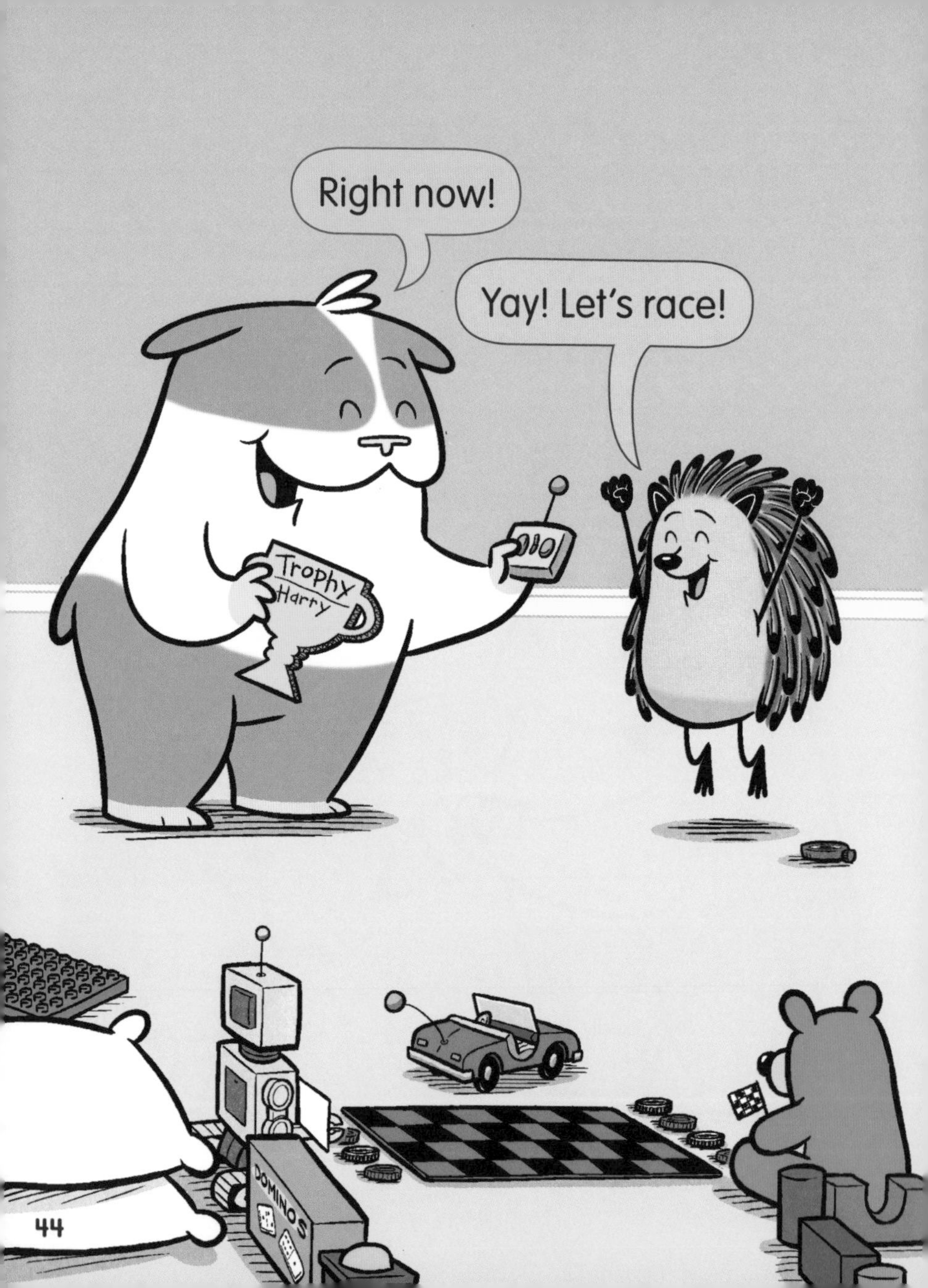
Right now!
Yay! Let's race!
Trophy
Harry
DOMINOS

About the Author

Norm Feuti lives in Massachusetts with his family, a dog, two cats, and a guinea pig. He is the creator of the newspaper comic strips **Retail** and **Gil**. He is also the author and illustrator of the graphic novel **The King of Kazoo**. **Hello, Hedgehog!** is Norm's first early reader series.

YOU CAN DRAW A CAR!

1. Draw a rectangle with round edges on top.

2. Draw three half circles inside the rectangle. Then draw a curved line to make the car's hood.

3. Add wheels! Draw four half circles below the rectangle. Then add a windshield on top of the rectangle.

4. Draw two headlights. Then add bumpers — one on the front and one on the back.

5. Add the seat. Draw details on the hood. Then add an antenna to the back of the car.

6. Color in your drawing!

WHAT'S YOUR STORY?

Harry races a toy car with Hedgehog.
Imagine Harry asks **you** to build a racetrack.
Where would you build it?
What things would you use?
Write and draw your story!

scholastic.com/acorn